BRIE'S SUBMISSION

In Sir's
Arms

Red Phoenix

Dedication

This has been quite a journey! I went from writing a simple short story, Brie's First Day of Submissive Training, to a series of sixteen novels to date—with spinoffs planned.

I couldn't have done it without my many fans. Your enthusiasm for the series inspires and humbles me.

I must always give special thanks to MrRed. He has not only inspired many scenes in the series, but he has been my number one supporter from the very beginning.

I give special thanks to my kids, as well, who have been proud and encouraging of their writer mom.

I would like to thank Anthony, who had a vision of how the series could continue, and has helped me move forward as an author.

Hugs to my son, who has taken on the marketing - love working with you!

Thanks to my dedicated proofers, Becki and Marilyn, who had to take on a crazy race to the finish.

Special thanks to Tanya for the special treat of WDW. It was magical.

YOU CAN ALSO BUY THE AUDIO BOOK!

In Sir's Arms #16

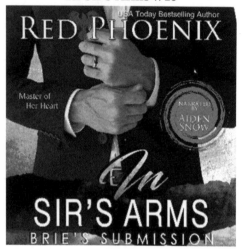

Coming soon…

Narrated by Aiden Snow

SIGN UP FOR MY NEWSLETTER
HERE FOR THE LATEST RED
PHOENIX UPDATES

SALES, GIVEAWAYS, NEW
RELEASES, PREORDER LINKS, AND
MORE!

SIGN UP HERE

REDPHOENIX69.COM/NEWSLETTER-SIGNUP

CONTENTS

Goodbyes

Thane felt a sense of foreboding overtake him as he looked down at Brie.

"I'd rather have you safe at home than have you fighting LA traffic," he explained, suddenly concerned for her safety.

She looked at him in surprise, unhappy that she would not be seeing him off at the airport but, to her credit, she did not protest. "I understand."

He smirked, knowing that although she *understood* his command, she did not agree with it. It was written all over her face even though she tried to hide it. Brie had never been good at hiding her emotions, but it was something that he loved about her. She was as genuine as they came.

Thane picked up his suitcase and headed toward the door, wanting to make a quick exit so it would be easier on them both, but he was suddenly overcome with an urge he could not deny.

He turned to face her, putting down his suitcase. In a formal voice, he said, "Before I leave, there are two things I must do."

She looked at him questioningly as he walked back to her. Thane growled in a low voice, "It's only right I give you a proper goodbye, Mrs. Davis." Fisting her long hair, he pulled her head back to plant a passionate kiss on those sexy lips.

Brie moaned in pleasure, melting against him. When he pulled away, she said with a flirtatious smile, "Thank you, Mr. Davis. I like proper goodbyes."

Thane then knelt down and grabbed her waist. The all-consuming feeling of love for the tiny being growing inside her surprised him. Pressing his lips against her stomach, he said, "Goodbye, little one."

He looked up at Brie and smiled. If he could have it his way, he would *not* be leaving today. He would have preferred to remain by Brie's side the entire pregnancy, but that would be foolish. As a businessman, he needed to take advantage of the rare opportunity he'd been given in Dubai. It was important that he continue to create a sound base of clients so that Brie and the baby were well taken care of.

Thane was not a man afraid of hard work but he liked to be efficient. Because of that, he'd been able to keep the time away from Brie to a minimum.

He stood back up, ignoring the nagging feeling of unease. Brie was safe, and that was all that mattered.

As the taxi drove him to the airport, Thane made a few calls to keep his mind focused on things other than his rising anxiety.

"Captain, I was instructed by Baron to call so we could set up a time to discuss your new project. Unfortunately, I'm headed to Dubai for the next four days, but why don't we set a meeting next week?"

"How does Wednesday at noon work for you?"

"I'm typing in my calendar as we speak."

"Excellent. Both Baron and I look forward to sharing our plans with you."

"And I look forward to hearing about it. Baron left Brie and I a cryptic message as a wedding present."

Captain chuckled. "He has been chomping at the bit to tell you for a while now."

Before Thane hung up, he gave into his misgivings and asked Captain, "Do you mind calling Brie while I'm gone to make sure she's doing well? Now that Brie is in a delicate condition, I feel...a tad overprotective."

Captained laughed. "Now, I must admit I never saw you as a doting husband but, then again, you never take on any job without giving it your full effort."

Thane chuckled self-consciously. "I'm rather shocked to find myself so concerned about Brie when it's only a few days, but there we have it. I acknowledge my concern and I own it. The fact is, knowing you'll be checking in on her while I'm gone eases my mind, since I'll be so far away."

"If such a simple request will provide you peace of mind while traveling, I'm happy to do it. Candy and I can even visit her if you'd like."

"You can ask Brie if she would like the company. I don't want my overprotectiveness to become a burden to her."

"As always, thoughtful and respectful to your woman."

Thane smiled to himself, thinking about Brie. "She deserves no less. Thank you, Captain. I look forward to seeing you next Wednesday."

Thane got out of the car, hopeful that the rising level of anxiety he'd been feeling would now dissipate. He walked through the crowded airport, finding he was acutely aware of the pregnant bellies and tiny infants he passed. He shook his head, amused that simply knowing Brie was pregnant was already changing his way of interacting with the world around him.

What the hell would he be like once the baby was born?

It's entirely possible Anderson has a valid reason for being concerned about us changing because of this child, he thought, chuckling to himself.

Thane boarded the plane and settled down, appreciative of his window seat. With the excessive amount of traveling he'd done throughout his career, there were times he felt claustrophobic sitting in the aisle seat. These days, he preferred the scenic view a window could provide, especially on the longer flights.

The stewardess sat a young girl in the aisle seat beside him. Normally, he would have groaned at the thought of dealing with a child for the next sixteen hours. However, his inner heart had changed, sparking a different response. He welcomed the challenge of it.

Thane listened to the stewardess explain, "Now, Lucinda, our pilot wanted me to give you this special pin." She promptly pinned a set of gold wings with the airlines logo onto the collar of the girl's dress and smiled. "It makes you part of the flight crew for this trip."

"Really?"

The woman nodded. "If you need anything, you just press this button right up here and one of us will come to help you."

Lucinda tried to press it with her fingers, her tongue sticking out from the concentrated effort, but she was too tiny to reach it. Seeing her reminded Thane of another little girl straining to reach for a bottle of catsup back when he was in college, and he chuckled. "Don't worry," he assured the child. "If you need to press the button, just tell me."

She looked at him shyly and nodded.

Thane could tell she was nervous, and why wouldn't she be at her young age—facing a plane ride in a huge, international plane full of strangers.

He held out his hand to her formally. "My name is Thane Davis. It is a pleasure to meet you, Miss…?"

She blushed as she took his hand. "I'm Lucinda Jefferys, mister."

"You may call me Thane, Miss Jefferys."

She looked at the stewardess and giggled. "He called me Miss Jefferys."

"I heard," the woman answered with a grin. "And you are in luck, Lucinda. Sir Davis happens to be a well-known instructor." When the little girl looked up at her, confused, the stewardess amended, "A teacher."

"Oh, like my teacher, Miss Honey?"

"Yes, but for older students like me."

When the stewardess shot Thane a glance, he realized she was one of the subs who frequented the Haven.

He nodded to her, letting the woman know that he

would look after the girl.

"So, Lucinda, do you like to fly on airplanes?" he asked, trying to distract her as she glanced around nervously.

She turned her head and looked up at him with big brown eyes. "This is my first time."

Thane smiled. "If it's your first time, then you should sit next to the window so you can see everything."

"May I?"

Thane unbuckled his seatbelt and grabbed his laptop from under the seat in front of him to make the switch. Once she was settled and buckled in, he asked her, "Can you see the men loading the plane with the luggage?"

"Yes, I can," she answered excitedly.

"See if you can spot your own suitcase as they load it."

With Lucinda's attention now on the stream of luggage being transferred onto the plane, Thane sat back in his aisle seat. He smiled to himself. There were times when small sacrifices were totally worth it.

A middle-aged woman sitting across the aisle commented, "It's nice what you did there."

He shrugged. "It's nothing for me, but everything to a first-time flyer."

"I heard the stewardess say you're a famous instructor. What do you teach?"

Thane smiled pleasantly. "Actually, I no longer teach these days. Instead, I help businesses run with more efficiency, hence my trip to Dubai." In order to change the subject and avoid any further questions about his past, he asked, "What has you headed to Dubai?"

The woman pointed to the man sitting next to her. "We're vacationing there because that city has all kinds of over-the-top entertainment like snow skiing inside a building, racing Formula One cars, and even diving with the sharks. But, me, I'm going for the full-body chocolate treatment and the 24-karat gold facial."

"Sounds decadent."

She grinned. "Only the best for me. So, other than business, what are your plans in Dubai?"

"Just there for business."

"Life is more than just work," she stated firmly.

Thane chuckled. "I had an old college roommate tell me the same thing, and you're both correct, but I have no time to play as I am anxious to return to my new wife." He looked down thoughtfully at the ring on his finger. It was more information than he had ever shared with a stranger, but just thinking about leaving Brie had him feeling uptight again.

He reasoned with himself. Brie was a grown woman and quite capable of taking care of herself for a few days. Why he was worried about leaving her was beyond him.

Hell, he chided himself, *you've got nine more months of this, buddy.*

The pilot came on over the speakers, announcing that they were about to leave and rattling off details about the flight. He ended his spiel by telling them to buckle in for a relaxing flight.

Thane turned to Lucinda. "Did you see your suitcase?"

She wore a worried expression and shook her head.

"That must mean it was already safely on the plane

before you started watching for it."

She smiled at him, nodding enthusiastically.

As they were taxiing, he watched her eyes growing wider in fear. To ease his own anxiety, and hers, Thane told the girl, "My favorite part of flying is when the plane takes off from the ground." He remembered when he was a boy, traveling with his father. "Have you ever wanted to fly like a bird?"

She nodded again.

"Well, now you will get to know what it feels like. It's fun," he assured her.

Her eyes flashed with excitement as she turned to look out the window again.

Thane stared past her as the engines began to roar and the large aircraft raced along the runway, slowly lifting off the ground.

The girl began bopping happily up and down in her seat. She looked back at him, grinning before pressing her nose against the window. Her enthusiasm for the takeoff was contagious and reminded him of the miracle that flight truly was. The fact that an aircraft carrying so many people, luggage, and fuel could break its connection with the Earth was extraordinary.

He wondered if this was a taste of what it was like to be a father. Seeing every aspect of the world in an entirely new way?

Thane looked at the girl and smiled to himself.

If so, he looked forward to reliving the wonder of the world through the eyes of his child. Just the thought of it had him tearing up, and he quickly swiped an errant tear away.

Just as they were banking right over the ocean, heading north, the plane was rocked by a loud explosion on the right side of the plane.

The moment Thane heard it, dread coursed through his body.

He had been wrong.

His anxiety had not been for Brie—it had been for his own fate.

Thane could see fire streaming from the engine on the opposite side of the plane and heard the frightened cry of the little girl beside him.

Remembering a study about the safest seat on a plane during a crash, he told her, "Lucinda, the pilot is going to get the plane back on the ground, but I need you to sit in the middle seat right now." He quickly unbuckled her and lifted her into the seat, buckling her back up.

With people screaming all around them, Thane looked into her eyes and said calmly, "You're safe. I will protect you."

She nodded with tears in her eyes, her bottom lip trembling.

Thane wrapped his arms around the little girl. He thought about his own child, who he would never meet.

Oh, Brie, you will need to be strong for her.

Her...

Thane felt certain their baby was a girl. A little girl who would never know him.

His heart broke.

Thane quietly repeated over and over to Lucinda, "You're going to be okay," as the plane pitched wildly, trying to make a last-ditch effort to land safely back at the airport.

He was determined to save this little girl—to make sure Lucinda made it out alive, even if he did not.

Random thoughts raced through his head in those last moments before impact:

Rytsar pressing his wrist against Thane's as they vowed to be brothers...

Brad's jovial face as he dunked Thane's head under the ocean water at the beach...

The pride he felt facing his first class of submissives as Headmaster of The Submissive Training Center...

His father's laughter as he lifted Thane up as a young boy, twirling him in the air...

The engaging smile of his mother as she pretended to catch fish on their make-believe pirate ship...

Throughout these memories, the sound of his father's violin steadily grew louder in his head.

Thane pulled Lucinda closer to him, covering her with his body.

His very last thoughts were of Brie and a recent memory of her—which were about to become a lifetime ago.

Shaking the mixture vigorously for several seconds, he poured the clear liquid out into two martini glasses and returned to Brie.

She gave him a questioning look as she took it from him.

"Drink," he commanded.

Ever dutiful, she took a small sip and broke out in a grin. "It's coconut water."

"As is mine. I will not ask you to do what I am unwilling to do myself," he stated. Holding up his martini glass, he said, "For our child."

Brie nodded and clinked glasses with him.

Thane had never known he was capable of feeling so protective of someone. The thought that Brie might be pregnant had him focused on her like never before.

She looked at him shyly. "Do you really think I could be pregnant so soon?"

Remembering all the passionate encounters they'd enjoyed over their long honeymoon, he replied with a smirk, "Wouldn't you say we've given it our best effort?"

She clinked glasses again. "We certainly have, Sir."

He took another sip of his mock martini and winked at her. "In answer to your question, I *do* believe you are already with child. The last couple of days, I've noticed a slight rise in your inner core temperature when we've been intimate, and your nipples have become unusually sensitive. Both are indicators of pregnancy."

"But it's only been a few weeks…"

"Of intense fucking," he reminded her lustfully.

When she looked up, her smile took his breath away. Brie had always had that power over him from the very first moment they met.

"Why don't you take a pregnancy test, my dear?" he suggested.

As Thane watched her walk down the hallway, he marveled at how Brie had been able to bring him to this place emotionally. Ever since his father's death, he'd closed himself off, only letting Rytsar into those darker parts of his soul.

He'd been satisfied to enhance the world with his knowledge of BDSM and keep his distance from everyone else. It was easier that way... safer that way.

Yet, here he was now, in love with a woman and ready to start a family with her.

Thane shook his head, still in shock at the turn his life had taken. Brie was proof that miracles were possible—that someone broken had hope for a normal life.

Hope...

Recently, that word had become like a mantra for him. Hope had not been a part of his reality since he was a young boy. It had had no place in his LBB—Life Before Brie.

When he heard her giggling nervously from the bathroom, he walked down the hallway and stuck his head inside the doorway. "Having problems, my dear?"

She looked up at him sheepishly from the toilet. "I'm too nervous to pee."

Thane turned on the sink faucet, knowing the sound of the running water would help. It didn't take long before she had the tester soaked. Laying the stick on the counter, they both watched it intently.

The first blue line slowly appeared, indicating that

the test was working. He waited with patience, certain the second blue line would soon follow.

Thane smiled when he saw the faint blue of that second line.

An image of his father flashed in his mind.

Papa, he called out silently, *I understand now...*

The full force of the burden of caring for this new life hit him hard, but along with it came an undeniable joy.

My child.

"Hello, little mama," he growled in Brie's ear, wrapping his arms around her.

She closed her eyes and purred. He looked at the reflection of the two of them in the mirror and mused.

This beautiful woman is going to have my baby.

He had to blink several times to hold back tears of gratitude.

Brie giggled. "Apparently, you were right. We *are* a compatible couple."

"No doubt my sperm enjoyed penetrating your egg."

She was silent, seemingly lost in thought. It was not the reaction he had been expecting. Turning her around to face him, he asked, "Are you okay, Brie? You're so quiet. You aren't having second thoughts, are you?"

She looked up at him, shaking her head with tears in her eyes. "No, I just can't believe I'm having a baby. *Your* baby, Thane."

His heart overflowed with his intense love for her and this new life she was now carrying. He crushed her in a tight embrace, murmuring gruffly, "*Our* baby."

The haunting melody of his father's violin overtook his thoughts while the sound of another explosion rocked the plane and it ripped apart around them.

"Goodbye, babygirl."

Hell

His universe was cold, dark, and excruciatingly painful. He was floating in a sea of pain without any way to end it—unable to move or react.

At first, Thane thought it was a dream and kept his insurmountable fears at bay with the belief that he would wake up soon. But the longer he waited for relief to come, the more uncertain he became that it would ever happen, until the fears he'd been fighting finally rushed over him, unabated.

Is this Hell?

All his life he'd heard stories about the fire and brimstone of Hell—but this was much, much worse.

Cold nothingness…

No sound.

No smells.

No light to see by.

Nothing to touch.

Floating in a bitter darkness, completely devoid of anything to hold on to.

A man could go mad in such an environment…

What had he done to earn this punishment?

Although Thane had been deeply wronged as a boy, he'd lived his life as honorably as he knew how, striving to protect himself and those around him.

Was that the reason he was here?

In protecting himself, had he earned a place in Hell?

Brie...

He screamed in agony, but no sound came from his lips.

Thane raged inside himself, furious that every part of his humanity had been stripped away from him but one—the ability to think.

What cruel irony.

With limitless time, and being of sound mind, he found himself reliving his past and questioning everything. All those memories only served to affirm his assumption that he'd been plunged into the cold heart of Hell.

~~~~~

Thirteen again...

He was headed up the walkway to the house, glancing at the unfamiliar car in the driveway, curious as to why it was there. Mama never invited guests over to the house.

Thane opened the door and called out to her as he hung his backpack up and took off his shoes, setting them neatly against the wall at the entryway.

Shoes were *not* allowed beyond that point. It would be a travesty to get those pristine white rugs dirty. Thane couldn't understand why his mother insisted on white, but he respected her wishes nonetheless.

A growing boy, he headed to the kitchen to round up a snack to satisfy his insatiable hunger. With a plate of chips and a hastily constructed sandwich, he made his way up the stairs to his bedroom. As he walked past his parents' room, however, he heard his mother's passionate cries.

Thane stopped in his tracks, horrified by the reality of what was happening behind those double doors.

She wouldn't...

Tears picked his eyes, and he suddenly felt nauseous. The plate in his hand fell to the floor unnoticed.

As if in a daze, he escaped into his room, terrified by his mother's betrayal.

"What do I do?" he mumbled as he paced the room. Should he go in and confront his mother, searing the image of her infidelity in his mind?

Tears of helplessness fell down his cheeks. He knew how crushed his father would be when he learned of her betrayal. Alonzo's love for his wife was so deep that Thane was uncertain how he would survive it.

Sitting at the edge of the bed, Thane held his head in his hands, rocking back and forth, certain his whole world was about to fall apart.

"Why?" he cried out. He could not fathom any reason his mother would do this to his father when she claimed to love Alonzo. They were like the sun and the moon—everyone said that about them.

Thane groaned as the faint sound of her sexual cries penetrated his thoughts.

"I can't deal with this!" he screamed out in a rage.

Racing from his room, Thane ran blindly past the double doors and down the stairs, slamming the front door on his way out.

He walked for hours, trying to reason out not only what had happened, but why it had happened. He understood his mother's loneliness. Hell, he felt that way, too, but they both knew that Alonzo was not only providing for the family, but also spreading joy around the world with his violin.

It made Thane proud, and it was worth the sacrifice.

No matter what his mother was feeling now, she owed her husband the respect of telling him about the affair to his face as soon as he returned home. Sneaking behind her husband's back to fuck another man in *his* bed was unconscionable.

Thane eventually walked back to the house, relieved to see that the car of his mother's "boy toy" was gone. When he walked inside, she was waiting for him.

"You can't tell your father."

"Don't make me lie for you, Mama."

"You don't have to lie. Just don't say anything."

"Lies of omission are still lies…" he growled.

"Do you really want to be the one who shatters this family?"

"I'm not the one who did this," he spat, disgusted that she was planning to hide her infidelity. There was no remorse on her face.

"Thane, you know I love your father," she insisted.

When he frowned at her in disbelief, she grabbed his arm and forced him to look her in the eye. "It's not right that I have to stay behind while he's traipsing all over the world, enjoying the adoration of millions of fans."

"Papa would never cheat on you."

"Whether he would or wouldn't has nothing to do with this."

"But it does," Thane snarled, "considering the fact you just cheated on him."

She smiled at him sympathetically. "You're just a boy and can't understand," she said in a soothing voice, tucking a strand of loose hair behind his ear. "If you love your father, you won't say anything about this."

Thane shook his head, shocked by her request.

When she saw the defiance in his eyes, she replied in a threatening tone, "If you do, whatever happens will be on you."

"I didn't betray Papa."

"Enough!" she shouted. "If you're so eager to destroy your father and watch our family shatter into a million pieces, then, by all means, tell him."

His mother walked away, grabbing her purse and keys. Before heading out the door, she turned around and stated coldly, "You left a mess in the hallway. I expect you to clean it up."

Any respect he had left for his mother evaporated the second she walked out that door. Ruth had put the burden of her betrayal squarely on his shoulders. It was a cruel thing to do to a young boy.

The one thing Thane was certain of was that his father deserved to know.

When Alonzo returned home, Thane watched in disgust as his mother acted as if nothing had happened, doting on her husband as she always had. His father's low laughter filled the house, suddenly causing Thane to doubt his decision.

He couldn't handle the thought of silencing his father's warm laughter with the ugly truth so, against his better judgement, he chose not to tell anyone...

~~~~~

Is that why I'm here? Thane cried out in the cold, black abyss. *Because it doesn't seem fair when I paid such a horrific price for that mistake a few years later.*

Without skipping a beat, the consequences of that decision played out in his head.

~~~~~

"There's no reason to push, dickwad," the boy in front of him grumbled as Thane forced his way off the bus.

He'd seen his father's Ferrari drive past as it pulled up to the house, parking behind the latest boy toy's vehicle.

No...no...no! he screamed silently.

The choking smell of exhaust fumes filled Thane's nostrils as he pushed his way off the bus and began sprinting toward the house.

His father had already opened the front door...

"Don't!" Thane cried out breathlessly, knowing he wouldn't be heard but desperate to stop what was about to happen. It was as if his legs had suddenly become lead, each step an incredible effort as he forced one foot in front of the other.

His father had no clue what he was walking into.

Heading up the stairs, grabbing the banister hand over hand to help propel him along faster, Thane saw the open double doors and knew he was already too late. When he entered the room, he stopped short—terrified.

His father had a gun pointed directly at his mother. The drawer by his bedside was open, its contents sprawled haphazardly on the floor.

Thane saw the naked "boy toy" lying in their bed, frozen in fear.

His father moved slowly, now aiming the gun at the asshole lying in the bed.

Alonzo said nothing as he vacillated between pointing the gun at one and then the other, a look of complete devastation on his face.

Finally, he lowered the weapon and asked his wife one simple question. "Why?"

She glared at him as if the circumstances had been reversed and she was the one who'd been wronged, but she said nothing in answer.

"Papa," Thane choked out.

Alonzo turned his head and stared at Thane for a moment. The look of raw pain in his eyes was something Thane would never forget.

"I'm sorry, son."

Before Thane could respond, Alonzo put the gun to his head and pulled the trigger.

Thane ran to him, screaming, as he watched his father's body fall limply to the floor. Reaching him, Thane cradled his head in his lap, ignoring the gushing blood and fragments of bone as he begged his father to hold on.

He looked over at his mother and yelled, "Call the fucking ambulance!"

Thane returned his attention to his father, startled to see his eyes blinking. Maybe there was hope he would survive. "Papa, you've got to hang on until the ambulance gets here. You're going to be okay."

Even as he said it, he knew in his heart it wasn't true.

Alonzo's gaze slowly drifted around the room until it finally locked on Thane.

"I love you," Thane choked out.

"Son…" His father blinked more and more slowly with each passing moment.

Thane was losing him, and there was nothing he could do.

"Don't die, Papa," Thane begged. "I need you…"

Alonzo's gaze did not waver. "*Ti amo.*"

Thane whimpered. "I love you, too."

His father stared at Thane with a look of unbearable sadness as his life slowly ebbed away. Thane held him tightly as he whispered his last words, "I'm sorry…"

His father's body stiffened, and Thane heard the horrifying sound of the death rattle as Alonzo took that final breath—the sound would haunt him forever.

At the tender age of fifteen, Thane watched in horror as the light disappeared from his father's eyes.

~~~~~

Looking back on that moment in this dark void, Thane could only condemn himself.

If he had confronted his father about his mother's infidelity when it first happened, it was possible Alonzo would still be alive today.

That thought devastated Thane. If only his father hadn't decided to surprise his wife and son by coming home early. Why was fate so cruel to the kind?

It wasn't until his father had passed away in his arms that Thane understood the disturbing reality of his future. The talented man who had so much to give the world was gone, and the woman whom he had spent his life devoted to had only one thing to say.

"Thank God I'm free…"

Instead of comforting her son, Ruth used his father's death as an opportunity to elevate herself in the eyes of the public while trashing Alonzo Davis's reputation. She then spent his fortune seeking popularity, neglecting her only child in her pursuit of fame.

Thane decided his mother had been aptly named. The beast was the personification of Ruth-lessness.

It dawned on him as he floated in the darkness that it might not have been the mistake of a young boy staying silent which had condemned him to Hell, but his deep rage against his own mother. He'd certainly spent his life killing her in as many ways as possible—in his mind. And she did die by his hands eventually, although he wished it could have been otherwise.

There had been several instances in his life when Thane had almost stooped to his mother's level, overcome by the demons surrounding him after his father's suicide, her betrayal, and her abandonment. He knew he was entirely capable of the same heartless actions as she was, since he was cut of the same cloth.

However, the compassionate soul of his father still resonated within him. Instead of becoming her equal, Thane chose the higher path.

Legally emancipating himself, Thane separated himself financially and emotionally from the beast, choosing to concentrate his efforts in making a name for himself in the business world—on his own terms.

Although he had sworn off women to preserve his sanity, his Italian blood demanded satisfaction. As much as he distrusted women on an emotional level, he was fascinated by their feminine bodies and took great pleasure in helping them discover their hidden desires.

With the encouragement of Durov and Anderson, he found a way to interact sexually without the emotional ties intimacy normally involved.

It was the perfect solution.

BDSM became his passion, and a new career path was born when he was appointed the Headmaster of the Submissive Training Center.

An image of Durov, bloody and battered, gagged and tied to his bed in the dorm room, popped into his head. That memory had always tormented Thane…

After the incident, he had been reluctant to visit his Russian friend, knowing he was partly to blame. After all, he'd been the one to introduce Samantha to Durov.

~~~~~

Thane had immediately noticed the chemistry between the two, even though both were highly dominant individuals. It had intrigued him to watch the sparks fly whenever Durov and Samantha were together. He had encouraged their growing attraction, curious as to how it would play out.

Thane never anticipated how it would end—yet, the guilt he carried still weighed heavily on his soul.

Durov had retreated into himself after the assault.

Thane understood why, having witnessed the level of abuse the Russian had endured after releasing Durov from his bonds to care for his many wounds.

Afterward, he had held the Russian in a protective embrace, silently horrified at how brutal Durov's assailant had been.

He was shocked to learn it was their mutual friend, Samantha, but knew justice must prevail and offered to take Durov to police to press charges. However, the Russian refused, and made Thane promise never to speak about it with others.

"I cannot bear it," he told Thane with tears in his eyes. "Everything that I knew myself to be has been stripped away. I am no longer a man."

"You are wrong, my friend. You are still the same man."

"*Nyet.* I grew up believing I was strong and could conquer the world—but now I see the truth. I am, and will forever be, a whipping boy."

It was like a physical punch to his gut, hearing Durov's words. "That is not true."

"It *is* the truth."

Thane grabbed him by the shoulders. "We determine our truth. No one else—not the world, not our circumstances, and definitely not those around us. *We* are in control."

"Are we?" Durov asked, doubt clouding his voice.

"I have lived my life holding onto that truth," Thane stated. "Because, if I am wrong…" He paused, the idea of it terrifying him. "…if I am wrong, then there would be no point continuing on."

"Exactly," Durov answered.

The hairs on the back of Thane's neck rose, hearing the finality in Durov's tone. "Suicide is not an option. It is *never* an option."

"Maybe for some it is."

Thane growled, the deep-seated rage he'd kept buried for years now swirling around him, whispering its hateful words. "Durov, you cannot let your mind go there."

The Russian looked him in the eyes. "It already has, multiple times. Do you not think I wanted to die when I found Tatianna drenched in her own blood? The only thing that kept me here was my mother. I could not bear to cause her that kind of pain."

"Then why would you consider doing it now?" Thane demanded.

"When people find out I was assaulted by a woman, I will become the laughing stock amongst my kin and a source of embarrassment for my mother."

"No one has to find out."

Rytsar shook his head. "The truth will always find light, no matter how fiercely we guard it."

Thane closed his eyes—the image of his father's face when he pulled the trigger suddenly being replaced by

Durov's. "It is cruel to place that heavy burden on others."

Durov tilted his head up questioningly, staring at Thane. "What about your own father?"

The blinding fury Thane had been trying to subdue erupted violently because of his simple, but loaded, question. Tears of rage rolled down Thane's cheeks as he screamed the forbidden words he'd kept buried all these years. "I hate my father for what he did!"

Thane turned away from Rytsar, trying to keep the gut-wrenching sobs from escaping, but he could not. The anger and sorrow flowed from him like a turbulent river he could not hope to control.

He felt Durov's strong arm wrap around him. "There, you have finally said it. I was wondering how long it would take."

Thane looked at him accusingly, furious with himself for having voiced it aloud, when he loved and admired his father so profoundly.

Durov nodded in understanding. "Your father killed himself in front of you. How could you not be angry?"

Thane shrugged off his friend's sympathy and stood up, walking over to the window. He needed distance from those unwanted emotions. In a voice ripe with pain, he admitted, "All this time I have run from the fact he committed suicide." Thane turned to face Durov, and asked, "Do you know why?"

"Because he was weak?"

Hearing Durov associate that word with Alonzo rubbed Thane raw, but he shook his head and told him the truth. "No. I live every day afraid that I will make that same choice."

Durov frowned, shaking his head adamantly. "You are the strongest man I know."

"I've thought a lot about it. If we are simply products of our parents and circumstance, like you insist, then I have one of two paths ahead. I will either become a monster, or I will die by my own hands."

Stillness filled the room as his greatest fear hovered in the air like a disease.

Durov met his gaze without blinking.

"I'm not okay with that," Thane stated angrily. "I choose a different path, but I have to fight to stay on it every damn...fucking...day."

Durov sighed heavily, nodding in agreement.

"Therefore, you must choose a different path, my friend—despite what happened to Tatianna, and despite what happened here. I guarantee it will be a hard fight, but I will be alongside you."

"I don't know..." Durov said, his voice raw with emotion.

"You must."

Durov shook his head, looking down at his hands. "When Tatianna committed suicide, I felt as if my life was over. I had no idea it could get worse."

Thane stated with complete sincerity, "If I could take your pain, I would."

Durov looked up, penetrating his soul with those intense blue eyes. "I would never wish it on you, but I appreciate the heart behind the offer."

"So you vow to fight?" Thane pressed.

Durov replied with a challenge. "If you will perform

the blood-bond with me."

Thane furrowed his brow. "What does it entail?"

"It is a vow of brotherhood. We promise our fidelity, protection, and comradeship to each other."

Thane felt a quickening in his spirit. The connection Durov was offering was the very thing he had longed for after the death of his father. It was as if someone had heard the cry of his heart and answered it with this burly Russian sitting before him.

However, Thane could not make that vow unless he was certain Durov would keep his promise. "If I agree, will you vow not to leave this world until your appointed time?"

"*Da*," he answered solemnly. "I give you my solemn vow not to rush my appointment with Death." He then added with a humorous shrug, "Unless, of course, shit really hits the fan."

Thane slapped him on the back. "You've had enough of shit for one lifetime. It's going to be smooth sailing from here on out."

"I hope you are right, comrade," Durov chuckled sadly, walking over to a large, wooden chest on the floor. He unlocked it and pulled out a dangerous-looking blade. "This will do."

Thane raised an eyebrow as he stared at the sizeable knife.

"We will not perform the ritual here," Durov explained. "It must be done at a sacred place."

"Like a church?" Thane asked, surprised.

"*Nyet*, but similar in nature."

"Ah, then you must mean the ocean."

Durov's eyes lit up. "*Da*, that would do."

"I know the perfect place then. Visited there many times after my father died."

"Even better. A place that has meaning for you. Tomorrow night, then?"

"No, tonight," Thane insisted.

Durov chuckled. "I approve of your Russian-like tenacity."

"What else do we need?"

"Alcohol, a strip of cotton, and this beauty," Durov answered, proudly holding up his blade.

Thane looked at the Russian, hoping this ritual commitment would give them the stability they both needed to connect on a deeper level. With Durov's passionate nature and his level-headedness, Thane was excited to see how far they could go.

For the first time, when Thane thought about the years ahead, they did not seem like a black hole. Thane could envision a life with balance, both predictable and rewarding.

And that had remained true—until he met Brie.

~~~~~

Thane found himself back in the tobacco shop.

With an amused smile, he asked the young woman, "Miss, could I have a pack of Treasurer cigarettes?"

When she turned to reply, Thane instantly became captivated by her honey-colored eyes, framed by those long, brown curls.

"I'm sorry. We don't carry those here."

Feigning ignorance of the shop his uncle managed, Thane looked around and stated casually, "Satisfy my curiosity and tell me what brand is in the box over there." He purposely pointed to a box just out of her reach.

She graciously bent down to open it up, and he was granted an enticing view of her shapely ass. When she turned around and caught him staring, she blanched and looked away.

Her reaction intrigued Thane.

The girl must have limited experience if she found it unusual for a man to be openly admiring that fine body of hers. It led him to wonder what else he might introduce her to.

The possibilities were endless…

"Do you like it here?" he asked.

Brie's eyes flashed with excitement when she answered, "Not exactly…" She glanced sheepishly at the back of the shop where his uncle must be working on inventory.

Her answer was all the permission Thane needed. While he was unsure if she would be open to exploring her submissive tendencies, he suspected she would prove an excellent student.

"You don't look as if you belong here," he stated, giving her a rare invitation to join the Submissive school by including his business card under the hundred-dollar bill he slid to her as payment for his purchase.

As he left the tiny establishment, Thane was overcome with a sense of providence.

He glanced back at the shop, certain now that the young woman would either prove to be his salvation or his utter ruin. The reason?

He'd felt an unexplainable connection to her the moment their eyes met. It both troubled and fascinated him.

~~~~~

Thane felt a crushing blow of grief knowing he was utterly alone now, stripped of Brie's love in this unbearable and unforgiving darkness.

It was as if this Hell wasn't simply satisfied to torment him with the past, but wanted to remind him of the future he had lost.

Mourning her as if she were dead, he retreated into himself, wanting freedom from all thought and emotion. In that inner silence, he heard her voice like a faint whisper on the wind. It was so soft at first it barely registered as sound.

Thane concentrated harder, begging Brie to speak again.

"Come back to me…"

Even though her voice remained impossibly faint, he heard the agony in her words.

Thane began screaming into the nothingness, demanding his life back. It didn't take long before he realized it was a waste of mental energy.

Instead of getting discouraged, he switched tactics. Concentrating all of his thoughts, Thane imagined physically digging himself out of the Hell he had been cast into. He did not deserve to be here.

His place was by Brie's side.

I AM...

With a sense of sheer horror, Thane made his way to the other side only to realize he was not only blind but completely paralyzed. The strange paralysis was cruel, because he could feel everything, yet was unable to react to stimuli.

He quickly concluded this was little better than the Hell he had just come from—except for two things. Although he had no control over his consciousness, when he *was* aware he could hear Brie clearly when she spoke.

More importantly—he could feel her touch.

She could not know how that anchored him in this terrifying new reality.

In this different version of Hell, he was a part of the world but could neither move nor respond to it.

Unwilling to give up, each time he regained consciousness, Thane forced himself to try to move every part of his body. He started with his fingers, trying to ball his hand into a fist, then he tried to move his wrists, and then his arms, trying to curl the muscle. From his neck all the way down to his toes, Thane concentrated on every muscle group, commanding them to move.

What he had learned about the brain in college, gave him hope now. The human brain was capable of making new connections when neural pathways died. It was truly miraculous, and gave Thane confidence that if he remained committed, he could retrain his body to respond.

The day that Brie leaned over and kissed his forehead, telling him she knew he was there and that she missed him, Thane wanted to shout to the rooftops and kiss her back.

Her gentle hands begin to caress his skin as she slowly and sensually bathed him with a sponge soaked with warm water. To feel her intimate touch was sensually arousing—reviving a part of himself he had lost in the battle.

She began with his feet, making sure to give every toe individual care and attention. When she was finished, he felt the warm of her mouth as she lightly sucked and then bit down on his big toe. "That's right, husband. I'm going to make slow, delicious love to your body as I bathe you…"

Even paralyzed, his body reacted to her sensual touch. He could feel the familiar ache begin to build in anticipation, as warm water cascaded down the calf of his leg when she gently sponged the length of it.

He would have groaned with pleasure if he could have made a sound.

After cleaning around his right leg which was covered in a cast, she began rubbing moisturizer into his skin. Her touch became like that of a masseuse as she stimulated his muscles, pushing hard while her hands glided over both his legs, inching ever closer to his upper thighs.

"You do know where I'm headed, don't you?" she growled lustfully, lifting his gown to expose his shaft.

She continued to work his leg muscles, grazing the crease between his leg and groin, but never blatantly touching the sensitive area. He felt the rush of blood as his body attempted to prepare itself to please her.

How unfortunate he could not.

Before she finished cleaning his pubic area, he felt the electricity of her lips on the head of his cock as she lightly kissed it.

Oh, what he wouldn't give to command her to continue.

Alas, he felt her lower his gown to continue his bath.

Thane appreciated the softness of her skin as she lifted his hand to her cheek. "I've always admired your manly arms, Sir. They contain such strength and demand so much of my body, and yet...your touch can also be gentle."

She placed his hand back down on the bed and purred in his ear, "I really love these hands."

Brie untied his gown and carefully lowered the material to run the wet sponge over his chest. He felt her trace the scar of the lowercase "t" with her finger. He was moved by the gesture, remembering the branding ceremony they had shared together.

"Condors forever," she whispered.

Brie then surprised him by taking his hand and tracing his finger over her own branding scar.

"Yours, Sir, until the end of time."

I love you, babygirl.

Brie leaned over and placed her warm lips against the brand on his chest.

"Now for your handsome face…"

She ran her hand over the stubble on his jaw. "As much as I love your facial hair, Sir, I need to give you a shave so you don't look quite so unruly."

Brie's soft laughter lifted his spirits.

With gentle hands, she spread a thin layer of shaving cream over his jaw. She had no idea how much he craved such simple stimulation.

The feel of the razor grazing his skin under her skilled hands, gave him pleasant chills. When she finished, she leaned over and left tiny kisses all over his newly shaven jaw. "So smooth and kissable…"

The last luxury Brie indulged him with was washing his hair. "You are a very lucky man, Sir, getting the full body treatment from a beautiful woman. Some men pay big bucks for this."

I would not only pay it—but tip you a thousand.

"Don't you love how it tingles? That's what you do to me whenever you run your fingers through my hair. My whole body gets the chills. It's heavenly."

He felt her warm breath as she whispered in his ear, "I need you to fight through the fog that consumes you. Follow my voice, Thane…come back to me." She kissed his cheek and went back to work.

I'm here, babygirl.

After his hair was washed, combed, and styled, Brie

told him, "You're one devilishly handsome man, Thane Davis."

She moved away, and he soon heard the sound of his father's haunting violin filling his ears. Then Brie lowered the bedrail and joined him on the bed, snuggling up against him while sighing in contentment.

Thane mentally groaned with pleasure. Even though he was stuck in this terrifying world between life and death, she had gifted him this moment of love and intimacy.

I will find my way back to you…

Brie was unwaveringly persistent in her mission to stimulate and encourage him in his recovery. She never stopped trying, day after day. The Dominant in him wanted her to rest and live her life outside this prison he was stuck in, but the man in him coveted her presence.

A few days after the sensual bath, she treated him to the latest entry in her fantasy journal. "Do you remember when you told me to write this, Sir? You didn't get the chance to read it, so I thought I would read it out loud to you now."

She caressed the page before beginning. "Just so you know, I was inspired by our Fiji experience…

"I lay naked before him as he gazes shamelessly over my body. Spreading my legs, he positions himself between my thighs. I turn away, not wanting to witness my descent into depravity, but he

turns my head back, making it clear I'm to watch.

"His thick white member pushes into my darkness. For a moment, I cannot breathe as his fullness takes over my reality.

"I cry out as he takes hold of my hips and pushes in farther. He grabs my wrists and begins to thrust. Chills overtake my body, making my nipples hard and tight.

"The ghost is inside me.

"I stare up into his blue eyes, surrendering my soul to him— my descent complete."

He heard Brie stand up and walk over to the bed, pressing her soft lips against his. She whispered softly afterward, "Wake up, my ghost."

Oh, how he wanted to tell her he was awake and aware. That all he wanted to do was reach up and pull her to him, kiss her deeply, and let his hands express how much he wanted her.

"Hello, Brianna."

Thane was shocked to hear that voice and howled silently.

Lilly.

Brie was clearly surprised, as well, the pitch of her voice rising when she answered, "Sir ordered you never to come around us again."

The woman ignored Brie, moving in closer. "I hear congratulations are in order, Mrs. Davis. It appears both you and I will be having a child of Thane's."

Thane silently yelled for Brie to run as he berated himself for never telling Brie about Lilly's blackmail attempt. He could only imagine the shock Brie was experiencing after hearing Lilly's accusation.

To her credit, Brie stated, "I don't believe you."

"The proof's right in front of your face. You and I both know what happened that night in China."

The bed shook as Brie gripped the railing.

Kick her out. Protect yourself!

Lilly's smooth voice filled the air with her lies. "I didn't come here for myself, Brianna. I'm here to protect the rights of my child—Thane's child. The honorable thing for you to do is to accept the financial responsibility you owe this baby."

Brie snarled in disgust. "I still don't believe you."

But Thane could hear the quaver of doubt creeping into her voice.

No, babygirl. Don't listen to her lies.

Lilly let out a condescending laugh. "Well, I've had a paternity test done. There is no question who the father is."

Thane knew Lilly had hit home with her lies when Brie did not respond immediately.

He raged within himself, furious that the bitch had successfully planted a seed of doubt in Brie's heart.

"I only expect half…"

And there is was. The only reason Lilly had come.

Brie, she's blackmailing you. Run away if you must.

"Half of what?"

"Half of whatever he leaves you in the will."

"Thane's not dead!"

Lilly answered with indifference. "He will be as soon as you turn off the ventilator. Serves him right for what he did to my mother—and me."

"Thane wouldn't—"

Trust that I would never do such a thing.

A chill like death enveloped Thane when Lilly whispered in his ear, "I'm back, Thane. What you did is unforgivable, and something you will pay dearly for."

Get the fuck away from us.

As if Brie could hear his thoughts, she ordered, "You need to leave. Now!"

"I give you two weeks to buy my silence, Brianna—after that, it's a free-for-all. It's the exact same offer I made Thane."

"What are you talking about?"

"He knows about the baby. But, apparently, he didn't tell you. Interesting… Why do you think that is?"

Thane felt his world fall away.

In wanting to protect Brie from Lilly's insanity, he'd left her unprepared for this attack, giving Lilly the opportunity to tear them apart.

After she left, Thane felt a distinct change in Brie. She wasn't with him anymore—not emotionally. He understood that she was now questioning everything she knew about him and their relationship—contemplating the possibility that he was as evil as his mother, and Lilly.

Not only had his half-sister effectively struck Brie down, but she had driven a stake through his own heart.

He heard Brie fall to the floor as he lay there like a statue, unable to help her.

This…this was hell.

Thane drifted in and out of consciousness. Without Brie's presence, there was nothing for him to hold onto. It would be easy for him to lose connection, drifting further and further away from reality without her.

Brie and the baby were his life.

I need you to come back, he called out, hoping she would hear the heartfelt plea of his spirit.

Time passed in the dark, unrelenting silence.

Then, like a miracle, he felt her touch again.

She took his hand and told him, "Seeing Lilly pregnant with a child she claims is yours has me questioning everything, Sir. Both Master Anderson and Mr. Thompson have advised me to keep my sights on what I know to be true. I am trying, Sir. I'm trying with all of my heart."

Brie then made a personal plea. "But...I need a sign from you. Something. Anything to let me know you're here with me now."

I am here, Brie.

He fought hard, commanding his body to move, begging it to move, and finally cussing at it, but...nothing happened—not even a twitch.

Brie let go of his hand, obviously disappointed.

Don't leave me, babygirl.

This was a do or die moment. He concentrated all his energy and thoughts into one powerful and simple command.

Open.

His eyelids obeyed, but he still found himself surrounded by darkness. Had he just imagined it? Thane cried out to Brie in desperation:

I.

Am.

Here.

His heartfelt cry was followed by cold silence.

Had he failed?

Suddenly, Brie's warm voice filled the room. "Sir!"

She was by his side again, clutching his hand and crying.

"Sir, can you see me?"

More silence followed when she realized he could not. To his profound relief, he felt a kiss as warm tears fell on his cheek.

"You opened your eyes for me!"

She then began kissing him all over, murmuring with joy, "You're here with me."

I am…

Awakening

Thane thought he had successfully fought and won his greatest battle—but he had no idea what was coming.

Although Brie knew he was there, Thane was still unable to see, speak, or move.

He might as well be dead.

Thane took courage from the fact he had been able to open his eyes. Surely, if that were possible, he would soon be able to move his hand or speak a word to Brie.

This vegetative condition could not be his fate…

He needed to hold Brie again and be there to greet their little girl when she came into the world.

What would be the point of surviving, only to live as a dead man?

Thane returned to his practice of concentrating on each individual muscle group, trying to get them to respond. As motivation, he listened to the constant ticking of the clock Brie had brought with her to the hospital room, believing:

Every second that ticks by is one less second that we are apart.

He was confident that his need to be with her was powerful enough to defeat this imitation of death.

Thane was aware of the presence of others in the room, mainly a woman with a soft voice and gentle touch, but he swore he heard familiar voices coming and going, as well—Anderson, Unc, Nosaka…

Unlike Brie's voice, however, theirs were not as succinct, sounding more like noise than speech.

All but Nosaka's.

When he spoke, it was as if the Kinbaku master was able to breach the barrier between them, reaching through the darkness to speak to Thane directly.

Thane was certain it meant he must be healing and would be able to wake from this nightmare, but he was wrong. The nightmare was about to get far, far worse.

It began so innocently while Thane was listening to the easy banter between Brie and Tono as they worked beside his bed. It had become a daily ritual of theirs, and it brought Thane comfort.

He felt a part of their daily routine even though he could only listen in. Hearing simple everyday chatter as Brie spoke of her film and Tono talked about his jute brought a sense of normalcy to this pseudo-death he was lost in.

Thane heard another voice in the room, and then Nosaka told Brie, "Hey, I'm headed to the parking garage for a bit. Seems someone hit my car."

"That's terrible, Tono!"

"I'm sure it's minor. I'll be back in a bit."

Brie was called out of the room soon after.

Thane couldn't explain the reason for it, but he felt

fear in the pit of his stomach, alerting him to the fact that something was terribly wrong.

When Brie returned, she seemed distracted and excitable as she explained to him, "Oh my gosh, Sir, I just had the most amazing stroke of luck! Some guy who works for Lilly is only a few blocks from here. He has Lilly's paternity test and evidence that it was manipulated. If I have solid evidence in my hands, Lilly loses all her power over us!"

He heard her place something on the tray beside him, followed by the sound of ripping paper. "Gotta take this with me or I might end up at the wrong place. Wouldn't that be tragic?" She broke out in giggles. "Oh, Sir, I can't believe this. We might finally be free of her!"

Brie gave him a quick peck on the cheek. "I gotta hurry. He said he's not going wait long."

None of it sounded right. Thane was convinced she was walking into a trap, and silently begged her not to go—but she ran out the door.

In his head, Thane was running after her and grabbing Brie before she made it another step farther. However, the reality was, he was lying there like an inanimate object.

A few seconds later, she was back, laughing.

He felt a flood of relief wash over him.

"Good grief, I almost forgot my purse. Be back soon!"

He heard her blow a kiss, and then she was gone.

Gone...

A cold chill fell over him.

Where the hell was Nosaka? Why wasn't he here to

stop her from leaving?

Thane lay in the bed waiting while his anxiety grew exponentially. Brie was headed for danger, and there was not a damn thing he could do about it.

To his relief, Nosaka finally entered the room. The man seemed frantic as he moved about the hospital room. Thane heard the sound of pounding keys as Nosaka searched her laptop, looking for clues to her whereabouts.

"Where are you, Brie?" Nosaka cried in frustration.

Thane knew she had written something down on the notepad sitting on his tray. Stilling his mind, he shot out one simple phrase like an arrow to Nosaka.

Tray.

He repeated it again and again, trusting the Kinbaku Master would be able to hear him beyond the abyss. But Thane felt a rush of despair when he heard Nosaka heading toward the door.

Thane shot the word out one last time, desperate to save Brie.

Nosaka stopped, and then Thane heard his footsteps returning to the bed.

"What's this?" he asked aloud, lifting the notepad from the tray.

Without another word, Nosaka hurried out of the room with Thane urging him on.

Thane's mind was exhausted from the concentrated effort and he slipped into the nothingness, drifting further and further away, consumed by dark visions and hellish screams.

"Sir Davis."

Thane heard Nosaka and centered his attention on the man's voice.

"Brie is safe."

Those words were like rain to his tormented soul.

"The baby is safe."

If Thane could have cried tears, he would have cried then.

"Thank you for your help, Sir Davis. I would never have found Brie if it weren't for the strong urge to look on the tray." Nosaka moved in closer. "I know it was you."

Thane would have rejoiced, knowing Nosaka had clearly heard him, if the situation had not been so dire.

In the midst of his solitary fight, Thane was given three gifts. The first was a vision of Brie that was so real, he felt as if he could touch her.

She was naked, smiling up at him from the floor, bound up in Nosaka's jute.

The joy radiating from her face was almost blinding.

In this dream world, he was a ghost, only able to observe—*but* he had the power of speech.

Looking at her, it seemed so real that Thane was convinced it was a glimpse into the future, and he was overcome with a profound sense of hope.

He spoke that word aloud and was startled when Brie responded, her smile growing wider as she nodded to him. Thane went to reach out to her and, suddenly, she was gone, although the feeling of closeness remained.

Thane lay there, listening to the clock ticking each second until they were together again, and it filled him with euphoria. The time of their reunion was near!

To add to his conviction that he was close to reentry into her world was the second gift.

The loud and passionate voice of Durov. It began with a scuffle between the bullheaded Russian and Nosaka, but ended with his friend pouring his heart out to Thane.

Accustomed to his disconnection from the world, Thane hadn't realized how much he'd missed the powerful bond between them.

"*Moy droog...*" Durov took his hand, clasping it firmly in both of his. He became silent for several moments, his voice broken. "We have been through too much, you and me. It cannot end here."

He placed his hand on Thane's chest. "You must do whatever it takes to return from the abyss. In turn, I promise to eliminate Lilly as a threat."

It amazed Thane that Durov knew exactly what he needed to hear.

"We share a similar story," the Russian continued. "You and I had endured more than most, even at our young age, by the time the two of us met."

He clasped Thane's hand again. "You helped me see beyond the hate and despair that filled my world, and I am eternally grateful for your influence." Durov then leaned in close to Thane's ear. "But here's the thing, *moy droog*. My darkness has returned, and the one man who could save me isn't here. I need you, brother."

Thane felt his pain as if it was his own. Rather than being weighed down by it, he added it to his arsenal, using it as motivation.

Durov is here.

Knowing that strengthened him, but Thane was gifted one more surprise—something he hadn't anticipated.

Brie burst into the hospital room a few days later, her voice bursting with excitement. "I just came back from my latest baby appointment and guess what, Sir? Rytsar recorded our baby's heartbeat for you! Here, let me play it."

Soon the sound of a rapid, steady heartbeat filled the room. Hearing that sound shot a bolt of energy through Thane and his heart began to race.

This was it, his bridge back to the living.

"He knows!" Brie cried to Durov. "Sir can hear his baby's heartbeat."

"Do you feel it, *moy droog*?" the Russian asked. "Hope is yours to claim."

Thane fought hard, commanding his spirit to make that final leap in conjunction with his body. He battled for what felt like an eternity, and just when he was on the verge of breaking through, his body gave out and he felt himself starting to slip away.

No!

Thane had nothing left to give and lay there utterly spent.

"What happened?" Brie whispered sadly. "He was so close. I could feel it."

I'm still here, babygirl.

Durov answered for him, "*Moy droog* needs time to rest so he can fight again tomorrow."

Thane's heart broke when he heard the disappointment in Brie's voice.

"It hurts…"

Don't give up.

Those words were as much for himself as they were for her. To be so close, and then to be pulled back into this pseudo-death, was almost impossible to bear.

Thane was convinced he had lost his only chance, that he would remain a shell of a man, when the name "Lilly" was brought up in a conversation between Durov and Brie.

"Rytsar, you've been so mysterious about Lilly," Brie said. "I believe you've found her, but…"

Hearing Lilly's name, Thane saw a vision of his half-sister—an exact replica of his treacherous mother—however, Lilly had a much more devious heart. All of the rage he'd held for his mother's many betrayals and Lilly's attempted blackmail and kidnapping boiled up to the surface.

It became an inferno of massive proportions.

When he heard Durov say, "If you knew what I knew, you would want her dead," it set off an explosion in Thane's mind. He concentrated on that fiery ball of hatred. Taking a lesson from Nosaka, he harnessed the immense power behind it.

Breathe!

Thane was blinded by a harsh light. Panic set in as he attempted to take a breath and suddenly found his lungs and throat on fire. His body became consumed by the life and death struggle for that much needed breath.

Brie's terrified screams filled his ears. "Fight this, Sir. Don't leave me!"

Thane refused to lose this time.

"Get her out of here," someone barked.

Brie held onto him tightly, dragging him with her as someone tried to pull them apart. Thane struggled, hearing Brie's cries as she was dragged away from him, but his body became wracked with pain as it fought to expel the object choking him.

A number of hands suddenly held him down, and he fought them off.

A woman's voice, which seemed remotely familiar, commanded him in a warm but firm tone, "Relax, Mr. Davis. We are trying to help."

Despite the overwhelming urge to keep fighting, he let reason prevail and stopped himself. In a matter of seconds, the skilled hands of the woman cleared his throat and he was able to take in a full breath.

The people around him began smiling and laughing.

The woman explained to him, "Mr. Davis, my name is Dr. Hessen. Blink your eyes twice if you can hear me."

Thane looked around wildly, bewildered by the painful brightness of the light and the numerous strangers around him.

"Mr. Davis, can you hear me?" she repeated.

Thane focused his eyes on her and blinked two

times.

"Good. I just took your breathing tube out, which is why your throat is sore."

He looked at her, wondering why she seemed so familiar when he was certain he had never met the woman.

"Mr. Davis," she continued, "you have been in a coma for the past four and a half months. Do you remember what happened?"

Thane blinked once, but his heart rate sped up as brief images of fire, a violin, and Brie came to mind.

"Don't be concerned. It's perfectly normal to have some temporary memory loss, following a head injury."

He looked to her for help, wanting to know exactly what had happened and how bad his condition was. The fact Brie was not in the room seemed an ominous sign.

Thane was afraid the physician would say he was completely paralyzed and that there was no hope for recovery. Instead, she said, "The other injuries you sustained in the accident have since healed."

Thane let out a long, labored sigh, closing his eyes as he took in that welcomed news.

"Would you like to see your wife?"

Although his body seemed to take far too long to respond, he blinked twice in answer.

"Wonderful. I'll bring her in."

Thane stared at the ceiling, uncertain if this was yet another dream sent from Hell to torment him, or if it truly was a miracle.

When he felt Brie's touch, he knew he was no longer in a dream. She lifted his hand and began covering it in light kisses.

Brie…

With immense effort, he managed to turn his head. When their eyes finally met, he felt a surge of relief and deep love for her.

Brie smiled at him, but with each passing moment, her expression of joy slowly became one of concern.

"Sir?"

Fighting the months of atrophy, he refocused his efforts, commanding his vocal cords to utter one word.

"Babygirl…"

Brie broke out in that beautiful smile he cherished. "Oh, Sir, I've missed you so much. So very much!"

Thane stared into her eyes, trying to express the relief and joy he felt. After a long battle in comatose Hell, he had finally broken the barrier that separated them.

He had made it back to her…

Thane noticed movement out of the corner of his eye and turned his gaze toward it.

Durov.

Thane stared at his friend with gratitude.

"*Moy droog.*"

Before Thane could manage a word, Durov held up his hand. "There is no need to say anything. You are back among the living." He hit his chest with his fist. "And your brother is deeply grateful."

Thane nodded slightly, a torrent of emotions building up with no outlet for their release. Durov, however, cried the tears of relief and celebration that he could not.

But there were darker emotions that rose up, as well. Feelings of anger, helplessness and concern for Brie and the baby. God only knew how much she'd endured the last four and a half months as he lay between life and death. There were so many emotions he could not express that it left him frustrated.

Durov made quick his exit, telling Thane, "I am stepping out for a moment, but do not slip back into a coma, *moy droog*. If you do, I will beat the shit out of you."

Thane would have laughed, but he could only manage the barest of smiles. Thank God for his stubborn friend. No matter how difficult the road to recovery, Durov would remain by his side, spurring him on while taking care of Brie. And, yes, Thane had no doubt if he slipped back into a coma, the burly Russian would hunt him down, even to the ends of the netherworld.

Before Durov left, he grinned at Brie and stated proudly, "Did I not tell you he would be fine?"

Brie's voice filled the room with joy. "He's back!"

Durov glanced at Thane and winked before heading out the door.

Brie smiled at Thane as she leaned over and kissed him tenderly on the lips.

Oh, the sweet taste of those lips… Thane groaned in pleasure.

With her face just inches from his, she said, "I have been waiting for this day ever since the plane crash." Her voice quavered as tears began to fall. "I never gave up hope."

Hope.

It was the recurring theme he associated with Brie. With great effort, each word coming out in a low, gruff whisper, he said, "I never…stopped…fighting."

She burst into tears, nodding her head as she took his hand and placed it against her cheek. "You came back to me."

Thane looked at her, wishing he could hold her tightly in his arms and tell her all the things he needed to say, but his body was uncooperative. He could only express with his eyes a fraction of what was in his heart.

Brie's honey-colored gaze shone with love, and he soaked it in—all of it.

He broke his gaze from hers for only a moment to look up toward the heavens. *If there is a God, I thank you for this second chance to be with her.*

He looked back at Brie. Nothing would stand in his way of recovering fully from this accident. No matter the prognosis he was given, Thane would continue to fight until he reclaimed the life he once had.

Looking down at Brie's growing stomach only added fuel to the fire. The baby needed a father who could protect and provide for her.

When Brie saw his gaze shift, she rubbed her belly and smiled. "Yes, our baby is doing well. Master Anderson, Tono, and Rytsar have all made sure of that."

His eyes darted back to hers in concern.

"Even though I never lost hope, I struggled for a while...so they stepped in," she explained.

Tears pricked his eyes.

She shook her head, smiling as she wiped away the one tear which escaped and ran down his cheek. "There's no reason to feel sad, Sir. Master Anderson made sure that I ate well, Tono encouraged me to work on my films, and Rytsar has been my protector ever since."

Despite her smile, he knew there were volumes she wasn't telling him and, based on the vague memories he could bring into focus, he knew some of it had to do with his half-sister. Thane had no idea which of those memories were real and which were only nightmares, but Lilly had been a constant theme throughout.

He was profoundly grateful for his friends, knowing they'd watched over Brie when he could not. Seeing her now, he appreciated that they had kept both Brie and the baby safe. He would never be able to thank them enough.

However, babygirl had a darkness behind her eyes he'd never seen before.

It stirred the Dominant nature in him. He had to recover so he could protect her, and take away the pain and fears she carried. It gutted Thane to be lying here, helpless, when he could see how much she needed him to be strong for her.

Thank God for Durov. He was the only person who truly understood the threat Lilly posed and could be trusted to eliminate the danger, should the need arise.

Although Thane was not a violent man, he would do *anything* to keep Brie and their baby safe.

Brie's hand grazed his cheek. "This is the happiest day of my life. Nothing could touch the joy I feel right now. I love you, Sir…"

She leaned forward again to kiss him.

Thane closed his eyes as the kiss lingered, and he expressed with his mouth how deeply he loved this woman. When she finally broke the kiss, her eyes crinkled into a smile. "I'd forgotten just how sexy those lips are."

He smirked weakly in response and tried to give her a witty reply, but that only ended up causing a coughing fit.

Brie instantly disappeared from his line of sight and returned a few seconds later with a cup of water, which she brought to his lips. "Drink this."

Thane took small sips and instantly felt the relief of the cold water running down his sore throat. Damn…he'd never realized how good water tasted until now. There was so much he'd been oblivious to.

He nodded to Brie in thanks when she took the cup away, not wanting to speak and possibly incite another spurt of coughing.

"Mrs. Davis?" Dr. Hessen said as she opened the door and walked into the room. "I'm sorry to interrupt, but there are some tests and assessments we need to perform."

"Of course."

Brie turned back to him. "Sir, would you like me to stay?"

He shook his head, saying in a hoarse whisper, "Durov."

She smiled, grabbing his hand and squeezing. "I'll see if I can find him." She leaned in for one last kiss, saying, "I'll be right back."

He felt a stirring in his heart. Those words, said so often while he lay in the coma, had meant everything to him.

"Brie," he croaked as she turned to leave.

She was immediately back by his side. "What, Sir?" she asked, her voice filled with concern.

"Love…"

Her bottom lip trembled. "I love you, too, Sir."

Brie had to drag herself away, and kept looking back as she was leaving. Before she exited, she pointed to her heart, crossed her arms over her chest, and pointed to him.

Thane nodded. He would never get tired of her telling him that, no matter how many different ways she chose to express it.

Stripped Bare

When Durov returned, he insisted on talking with Thane alone.

There was no doubt the discussion had to do with Lilly, and Thane was impatient to find out why Brie had been drugged, since Brie had been vague about it.

His brother picked up the chair beside the bed and turned it backwards before sitting down. "We have much to talk about but, first...before anything else, you must know I would have been here the instant I heard about the crash. But there's the catch, I was not informed about the accident until only a few weeks ago. Whether it was a legitimate mistake or by design, I am still not sure, but know that my absence was not of my own doing, *moy droog*."

Thane shook his head. He couldn't fathom why Durov wouldn't have been the first one called and looked at his friend with concern.

Durov saw he was upset and quickly laughed it off. "In the end, it is not important because I am here now, *radost moya* is safe, and you, comrade, are wide awake."

Thane glanced toward the door Brie had just exited, feeling apprehensive.

"*Da*, it is serious, *moy droog*. Your creature of a half-sister planned to do Brie and the babe great harm."

Thane looked back at Durov, alarmed when he hesitated to say more. It was unlike the passionate Russian—his silence was ominous. "This woman deserves to die, and we both know she will continue to be a threat to you both until she draws her last breath. With forceful persuasion, I have gotten her to confess several key things. Are you interested in hearing them now, or would you rather wait until you have had a few days to recover?"

Thane would have punched Durov, if he'd had the strength. Instead, he was left glaring at his friend, waiting for him to speak.

"Very well, but I warn you, such knowledge may prove a hindrance to your recovery, for to know such things and not be able to take action is detrimental to the soul."

Without hesitation, Thane forced out the words, "Tell…me."

"You have been warned…" He leaned even closer, speaking to Thane in low tones to keep the conversation private, should someone walk in. "She's truly depraved, comrade. When she met you the first time, the creature found you extremely attractive, dismissing the fact you both share a mother."

Thane was sickened by the revelation and looked at Durov in disgust.

The Russian shared how Lilly had come to be with

child, explaining, "The man she was having an affair with resented her for wanting to break up his marriage, and became violent when she tried to blackmail him. Knowing she could not go to the police after the attack, she crafted a plan to ensnare you—the true object of her obsession. When you joined her in China, she'd already set in motion her trap for you. But, *moy droog*, as depraved as she was, claiming the child was yours, it is nothing compared to what she tried to do to *radost moya* and the babe."

Thane stared at him, unsure if he could handle what Durov was about to say.

"The creature knew you to be a gentleman, and she convinced herself that you would insist on raising the child as your own after her false accusations. And, given enough time together, you would fall in love with her."

Thane narrowed his eyes, shaking his head. The story Durov told was beyond anything he could have imagined.

"I agree the creature is warped in the head, and I could have had a level of sympathy for her, but for what came next."

Durov got up and started pacing. Thane watched him with growing concern as the man paced back and forth in silence. His comrade had suffered a myriad of horrific experiences in his life, which left Thane dreading what had him so upset now.

Sitting back down, Durov looked at Thane, his whole being tense with rage. "The creature had your woman drugged so that…" Durov closed his eyes, fighting to say the words out loud. "She planned to kill *moye solntse.*"

Ice ran through Thane's veins, seeping into the depths of his soul. He'd never thought her capable of murder.

"But that was not all." Durov's eyes welled up with tears as he continued. "The creature had already sold Brie into slavery and was going to have her delivered into the hands of a monster after the loss of the babe. A life like Tatianna's, but so much worse…"

The devastation on Durov's face matched his own. Thane fought back the dark rage that was mounting—ready to consume his soul.

"*Moy droog*, I regret that I am not able to eliminate the threat while she remains with child, and you can only lie here with the knowledge of what she tried to do."

The Russian stared at his palms, looking gutted. "Both of our hands are tied for different reasons."

The horrific truth was worse than anything Thane could have imagined. He struggled to digest it, the bile of how truly monstrous Lilly was proving impossible to swallow—as was the realization of how close Thane had come to losing everything he loved.

In the past, Durov had leaned heavily on Thane during critical points in his life, but now their roles were reversed. Thane needed Durov to be his strength.

Thane stared at him, lost in a feeling of helplessness, and whispered hoarsely, "Brother."

"Why didn't you tell me sooner, *moy droog*?" Durov accused him. "I could have squashed the creature before she had the chance to harm anyone."

Thane was devastated by the question and could say

nothing, knowing his silence had almost cost Brie her life.

Durov shook his head. "Actually, I am not being fair to you…"

Thane's eyes narrowed, realizing his friend was hiding something more.

Durov sighed deeply. "I am also guilty of keeping things from you in an attempt to protect *radost moya*. Like true brothers, we share the same flaw."

Thane frowned, squeezing his friend's hand—demanding an explanation.

The resignation on Durov's face when he met Thane's gaze was disquieting. "*Moy droog*, the situation involving the maggot I killed has become…complicated. The Kozlov brothers are seeking revenge because it turns out he was their second cousin once removed. Although they'd never met in person, it became a convenient excuse for vengeance against me."

Thane nodded slowly, the cold realization of how dire the situation really was now becoming apparent.

"I thought I was safe, but now I see the tides turning and I cannot stop what is coming." He slapped his other hand against Thane's and held it tight in both hands. "But I promise with every breath still left in me that I will not let *radost moya* suffer for what happened in Russia."

Thane stared at him, unable to process it all.

Durov slapped his shoulder encouragingly. "The Kozlov brothers desire my death as payment for the maggot. I vow not to go down without a fight but, if the worst should happen, do not mourn for me. I will be with Tatianna, and will sup at my mother's table again."

Thane understood how dangerous the Koslovs were, but his friend was speaking as if he'd already given up hope of escaping.

Thane would not, could *not,* accept that this was his fate, and spat out a word, throwing down the gauntlet. "Coward…"

Durov smirked, accepting his challenge. "Fine, you peasant bastard. I will fight as hard as you have. We are brothers, after all. Stubborn to the depths of our dark souls."

Thane stared at him, expressing with the force of his will, one single, driving thought:

I canno't lose you, brother.

Thane had not appreciated at the time that Durov suspected what was coming and was actually telling him goodbye.

To have his brother physically dragged out of the hospital room by the *bratva* to be tortured and killed that very next morning was beyond what Thane was capable of bearing.

He lay there in utter shock, listening to Brie's sobs, as the room was flooded with strangers asking him questions he was unable to answer.

Thane held out his hand to Brie, holding her tight as he closed his eyes and tuned out the world.

This cannot be his fate.

Thane suddenly screamed, shutting up everyone in the room. They slowly filed out, leaving the two of them alone. The silence left behind was deafening.

"He's going to come back," Thane assured Brie. He said it not because he believed it, but because it had to be true.

Any other reality was not acceptable.

What little he knew about the Koslov brothers he'd learned from Durov. He understood they were a powerful faction of the Russian *bratva* and were feared in their country. Thane needed to learn more about them so he could get Durov back alive. Bribery was a powerful tool, and if placed in the right hands, it could open doors nothing else could.

Thane needed to contact Durov's four brothers and enlist their help. Although he had no respect for the men because of their contemptable treatment of Durov, Thane would have to rely on their assistance to have any chance of rescuing him.

Only a blood relative would be able to negotiate with the Koslovs.

Thane would approach Timur first, remembering that Durov had mentioned he was the most reasonable of the four.

Titov was another good option...

If Thane could keep his head straight, he was confident he could devise a plan to get Durov back. But time was of the essence.

The door opened, interrupting his thoughts, when Wallace entered the room. The boy seemed harried and overly nervous as he approached.

"I…I'm sorry to disturb you both."

Brie looked up at him and complained weakly, "But I told you not to come."

"I know," Wallace said, looking at Thane as he answered. "However, I'm here to speak to you on the orders of a mutual friend."

Thane narrowed his eyes, certain the boy was speaking of Durov. "Come…closer."

Wallace stood next to Brie, speaking in quiet tones. "I have news about Lilly."

Thane saw Brie's face drain of all color.

"Durov spoke with me yesterday. Together, we formulated a plan to get Lilly behind bars as quickly as possible."

Brie broke into tears, too fragile to handle anything more.

However, Wallace was insistent, and thankfully so. "I came to inform you that she has been arrested and is in jail. I made sure, personally. I wanted you both to rest assured that she is no longer a threat, and I will continue to monitor her situation to guarantee it remains that way."

"You should not—" Sir began.

Wallace interrupted. "Durov asked me to manage the situation, and that is what I will do—without fail."

Brie's voice broke. "You…saw him…yesterday?"

"Yes, Brie. I vowed I would protect you if he could not."

She looked crestfallen as she whimpered, "He knew this was coming?"

Thane held out a shaking hand, placing it on Brie's.

She instantly quieted, comforted by her Master's touch, but the tears continued to fall.

"I'm here for you both in whatever capacity you need. I owe you my life."

Thane shook his head. "You owe...nothing."

Wallace vehemently disagreed. "You found my donor on the other side of the world when I'd all but given up, and Brie cared for me in the hospital—even making sure I had chocolate." He met Thane's gaze, adding, "I remember when you told me 'There are families formed by blood, and others by character.' Well, you guys, and that crazy Russian, are now part of my family."

Brie lowered her head and let out a quiet sob.

Thane felt a punch to his chest as he relived that moment when Durov's unconscious body was dragged out of his hospital room by Koslovs' men. "We are both...still in shock."

"Is there anything I can do to h—"

A familiar voice came bursting through the door, stating emphatically, "Of course he wants to see me. And even if he didn't, nothing would stop me."

The nurse following behind, apologizing to Thane. "He wouldn't take no for an answer!"

Anderson ignored everyone else in the room, breaking into a wide smile when he saw Thane. "It's a damn good sight to see those eyes open, buddy."

"Master Anderson," Brie cried, melting into his embrace as she laid her head against his broad chest. Anderson wrapped his arms around her in a bear hug as he lifted Brie off the floor, and carried her back over to Thane.

He looked at Thane, shaking his head, as he set Brie down and grabbed him in a muscular embrace.

Thane closed his eyes, soaking in Anderson's strength—needing the power of his friendship to navigate what lay ahead.

When Anderson let go, he wiped his eye and pointed a finger at Thane. "Damn it, man. You gave us all quite the scare. Don't be pulling that shit again, buddy." Anderson looked over at Brie and added, "Neither she nor I can handle it."

Thane stared intently at Anderson's legs with a raise eyebrow, having heard about the car accident. "No…more…crashes."

Anderson chuckled. "That's a deal. No more crashes for either of us." He made a wide sweeping motion with both his hands. "Ever."

Brie let out a sad laugh. "I've had enough scares to last me *two* lifetimes."

Anderson put an arm around her and winked. "Didn't I tell you he would be okay, darlin'?"

"You did." Brie looked at both Thane and Wallace, and said, "He never gave up believing Sir would recover, and he was unwavering in his belief in his innocence, no matter how calculated Lilly's accusations became."

Brie turned her attention back on Anderson. "You helped me hold onto the truth."

Thane stared at his old college friend, unable to express the gratitude he felt. He'd heard from Brie how unfailingly loyal Anderson had been, not only to him, but to Brie herself. Even though Thane's speech was limited, he yearned to express how grateful he was for their friendship, and summed it up in one simple word.

"Buddy."

Anderson shook his finger at him again, tears in his eyes as he grinned. "You got that right, bud."

It wasn't until then that Anderson addressed Wallace, his tone hostile. "Explain to me exactly why *you* are here."

Thane attempted to explain. "He's helpin—" Unfortunately, the effort caused him to break into a violent fit of coughing.

Brie immediately grabbed a cup of water from the tray and tipped it up, helping him to drink. She turned to the other men and insisted, "We have to keep our questions to a simple yes or no."

Anderson nodded, looking concerned as the nurse rushed in to check on Thane.

After she left, Wallace asked, "Do you know where they took Durov?"

Thane shook his head, upset he had no answer. Durov had once shared that the Koslovs were famous for making people disappear.

"Is there someone you need us to contact?" Anderson asked.

He nodded, his heart racing, knowing that time was ticking away.

While they continued to ask yes and no questions, it quickly became apparent to Thane that Anderson had been left out of most of what was going on.

The man was none too pleased about it and took it out on Wallace.

"Look, Anderson, I wasn't Durov's first choice, by

any means," Wallace replied in a defensive tone.

Anderson shook his head, growling. "I don't get it. I would do *anything* for you both. Why was I kept out of the loop?" He closed his eyes for a moment and then sighed in frustration, muttering, "That sadistic bastard…"

While Thane could not explain what was going on between Durov and Anderson, he didn't have time to concern himself with it. Top of his list was reaching the Koslovs with an offer they could not refuse.

"Call Titov," Thane commanded, his throat painfully hoarse after coughing so hard.

Wallace dialed the number, but shook his head afterward. "His number is no longer working."

Thane frowned, the feeling of desperation eating at him.

"Why is the phone disconnected. What does it mean?" Anderson asked Wallace.

"They are all…in danger," Thane answered.

"All of them?" Brie cried out.

Thane could not spare her from the truth. "Koslovs are ruthless."

He heard the worry in Brie's voice when she asked Wallace, "Do you have any other way to reach him—anybody?"

He shook his head sadly. "No. As far as I am aware, there was no backup plan."

"Damn…" Anderson muttered. "But they all can't have vanished into thin air."

"They must to survive," Thane informed him.

Brie looked at Thane in desperation. "What do we

do now?"

Thane struggled to sit upright, determined to help his brother, but his body was too weak. His attempt only caused another bout of coughing, leaving him weak and out of breath. "I have to get out of this damn bed." He tried again, but only succeeded in starting another round of coughing.

The nurse ran in, concerned.

"Sir's pushing himself too hard," Brie explained.

"I have to get out of bed," he stated, looking to the nurse for help.

"I'm sorry, but that's going to take some time," she answered. "You need to rest."

"I don't have time!"

Thane glanced at Wallace and Anderson, the fear and desperation he felt impossible to hide. "He cannot die."

Thane made the call to Timur after he'd had time to collect himself. In his condition, even a short call would take great effort, but he steeled his mind for the task, determined to bring Durov home.

Timur's number was the only one he had of the brothers, kept under the name "Tammy", in case Durov ever got hold of Thane's phone. He knew of the bad blood between them, but being a prudent man, Thane had kept the contact number in case of an emergency. He never thought he would ever have to use it.

Speaking in Russian, Thane explained to Timur who

he was and why he was calling. He was surprised by the cold reception he received.

"I have no interest in helping Anton."

Thane was shocked. When he tried to explain the dire situation, the man refused to listen.

"Can I have the numbers of your siblings?"

"*Nyet*. They feel the same as I."

"This is a life or death matter," Thane insisted.

"Fine, you may have Vlad's, but he disowned Anton long ago. He will not help, I guarantee it."

Before Thane let him go he felt the urge to ask, "Have you never questioned it?"

"What?"

"Whether Anton deserves your wrath?"

"Do not speak to me again," Timur stated, hanging up the phone.

Thane didn't skip a beat, calling Vlad next. He met with the same resistance, although Vlad was more vocal about his hatred of Durov. Unlike Timur, he freely gave out his brother's numbers. "It won't make a difference what you do. They already offered a ransom and I turned it down."

Thane stared at his phone in shock as he set it down. Vlad, oldest of the Durov brothers, had turned down the only chance of getting Anton, his own blood and kin, out alive.

How was that possible?

Thane glanced at Brie, who obviously knew something was wrong, but was too afraid to ask him about it.

For the first time, Thane began to doubt he could save his brother. He lay there with the knowledge that his friend was headed to certain death and there was nothing he could do about it.

Thane picked up his phone again and called Wallace. He'd mentioned speaking to Durov the day before. It was possible he might have information Thane could use.

"Can you come back? We need to talk."

Stolen Moment

Knowing him well, Brie found a way to empower them both during this uncertain and difficult time for them. Returning to his room after speaking with the nurses, Brie took his hand and explained with a coy smile, "I just had a conversation with Miss Abby, and she agrees. It's important that I love you."

"Meaning?"

"Well..." She playfully ran her fingers against the rail of the bed. "I had to promise not to barricade the door, but she gave her solemn promise that we will not be disturbed for the next hour."

"An entire hour?"

"Yes," she whispered seductively. "And I was thinking about how much I miss those long sessions of pleasing your cock with my mouth."

The instant those words escaped her luscious lips, Thane felt the familiar ache of desire.

Brie's eyes drifted down as she licked her lips suggestively. "What would you think of schooling me for the next sixty minutes, Master?"

"I think you should lower this railing and strip for me, babygirl."

The excitement in her eyes as she slowly lowered the rail and backed away from him stirred the Dominant in him. It had been far too long since they had been together intimately.

The way she swayed her hips back and forth as she began to unbutton her blouse reminded him of the first time she'd stripped for him at the Training Center after a formal lesson by Mr. Gallant.

At that time, he'd been impressed by her enthusiasm and desire to please, but it was that smile, her fine ass, and the undeniable chemistry between them, that had truly captivated his heart. At the time, he had tried to hide his growing attraction from her and his colleagues.

Although he'd been successful for the most part at keeping his emotions toward Brie a secret, Gray had seen through his carefully crafted façade, calling him on it right from the very beginning.

"Sir Davis, may I have a word with you?"

Thane knew from the tone in the trainer's voice that Marquis was not asking, but insisting.

"Certainly. Let me finish up my paperwork and we can talk on the way out."

"Very well," Gray replied, his tone carrying a harsh note behind it.

Gray had wanted to dismiss Brie's application after

seeing her entrance video because she'd moaned the name "Sir" several times throughout it. Gray claimed there was a relationship already established between them, which was strictly against the Center's policy.

Thane had been thoroughly insulted by Gray's accusation, and stood behind his assertion that she was a stranger to him.

Master Coen had taken Gray's side and agreed her application should be excluded based on her obvious attraction to the Headmaster. Thankfully, Samantha had prevailed, championing Brie's inclusion into the program by stating that the girl's natural curiosity and submissive nature made her an excellent candidate. She stood firmly behind Thane's recommendation, convincing the rest of the training staff that Brie would not only benefit greatly from their program, but that she should be granted an exclusive scholarship.

Due to Samantha's skilled arguments, she was finally able to sway the vote and Brie was officially admitted into the program against Gray's better judgement.

It was a victory, but based on Gray's tone just now, Thane knew he was in for a long battle ahead.

With an exasperated sigh, Thane got up from his desk and walked out of the office, locking the door behind him. As expected, Gray was waiting impatiently in the lobby.

"Let me get straight to the point."

"Let's," Thane agreed without hesitation.

"It's obvious that Miss Bennett has feelings for you, so please explain to me why you escorted her to your office while class was still in session tonight?"

Thane raised an eyebrow, resenting the insinuation that he had acted unprofessionally. However, he had to hold back his indignation, because Gray was correct on one point. Although Thane had acted professionally, he *did* plan to take the young woman's anal virginity tomorrow during class, and had told the girl as much.

Thane couldn't deny that he was attracted to Miss Bennett and that shapely ass of hers. He'd envisioned taking it ever since their chance meeting at the tobacco shop, and he'd be damned if he would let Gray interfere now.

He knew with certainty that, once that carnal desire to claim her virginity was satisfied, he would easily fall back into his role as her impersonal trainer. It was simply a matter of lust, a desire that needed quick release. The sooner he satisfied that desire, the sooner he could move beyond it.

Besides, Thane reasoned to himself, the girl deserved her first experience to be in the hands of an expert. It was only appropriate, being Headmaster of the school, that he be the one to handle the responsibility. He had no doubt that he could get the other trainers on the panel to agree.

In response to Gray's accusation, he explained, "I'm sure you noticed that Miss Bennett was distracted near the end of class. If I had not taken her out and spoken with her privately to assess her thoughts, it would have been irresponsible on my part as her trainer *and* as Headmaster of the school."

Gray understood Thane held the power because of his position and countered with, "May I suggest, then, that you allow others on the panel to handle dealings with the young woman?"

Thane stopped walking and turned to face Gray. "I am quite capable of keeping a professional distance with my students. Have I not proven that time and time again these last five years?"

"Yes…" Gray agreed, inclining his head toward Thane. "Until now."

"Why do you insist on looking for trouble where there is none to be had? I find it extremely insulting."

"So you have said, repeatedly. However, I feel thou dost protest too much."

"Just say what you mean," Thane growled irritably.

"The more you assert that you have no designs on the girl, the less I am inclined to believe you."

"I'm not the one constantly bringing it up."

"If things are as you say, we won't have an issue. But know this, Sir Davis, just because Miss Bennett has a submissive spirit, does not give you the right to take advantage of her. If you do, there will be severe consequences. Our duty is to the student, not our own selfish desires." He glanced at Thane's crotch for emphasis.

It took everything in Thane not to rip into the man, but he had found through experience that the harder people pushed, the better it was not to react. It was a calculated response on his part.

Verbal attacks often ended when Thane refused to engage. It also gave the individual a false sense of victory, while leaving Thane time to think further on the issue. If it turned out that the person truly had a valid point, Thane would not have to come back later and apologize for reckless words said in the heat of the moment.

With this particular situation, however, the more the man goaded him, the more determined Thane was to be the one to claim Miss Bennett's anal virginity.

No one was going to stop him, especially Gray.

Instead of scening with her on stage in front of the panel during the practicum as he had originally planned, Thane made the decision to meet with Miss Bennett alone—after class.

Thane liked the idea of being the only one to hear the beautiful Miss Bennett crying out his name repeatedly as he slid his cock deep into her virginal ass…

Thane refocused his thoughts on Brie as she continued her sensual striptease for him, exposing ever more of her irresistible body.

Thane remembered how he'd fought with righteous indignity against Gray's accusations during her entire training, only to discover at the Collaring Ceremony that the man had been correct all along.

Brie was not the only one compromised during their first meeting. The truth was, the minute he walked into that tiny tobacco shop, he never stood a chance.

She turned away from Thane as she let her blouse fall to the floor, smiling back at him as she did so. "Do you like what you see, Master?" Brie asked in an innocent voice while wiggling that sexy ass of hers.

"You know I've always admired that delectable body."

Brie giggled, turning around to expose her bare belly to him. Seeing it was a jarring reminder of how much time had passed—how much he'd missed. He struggled to keep the feelings of regret from his face, but Brie instantly abandoned her striptease as she rushed over to him. "What's wrong, Sir?"

Not wanting to ruin the moment, he smiled at her lustfully. "It's been so long…I may not last."

Brie licked her lips in a suggestive manner. "I don't mind, Master."

Thane watched as she grasped his cock with her hand and those perfect lips slowly descended on his needy flesh. Fighting the urge to close his eyes, Thane groaned as the warmth of her mouth encased the entire head of his shaft.

"Fuck me…" he groaned with a satisfied sigh.

Brie looked up at him, breaking the seal of her lips momentarily. "That's what she said."

Thane chuckled as he pushed her head back down.

Over the span of two years and after hours of thoughtful training, Brie had acquired the skills of an artisan. Her knowledge of his sensitive areas and her natural ability to read him meant that she could bring him to the edge and ease him back down repeatedly.

It was pure, masculine heaven.

He eventually closed his eyes, so he could fully enjoy the feel of her throat's constriction as she took him more deeply.

Her expertise in providing the perfect suction, flick

of the tongue, and sensual pressure drove him absolutely wild.

"I have missed this…" he growled lustfully.

She moaned in agreement, keeping that lovely mouth on his cock.

When the hour was almost up, he commanded, "Rather than come deep in your throat, I would like to come in that hot pussy of yours."

Brie pulled away, wiping her mouth with a grin. "That would be my greatest pleasure."

She pulled over a chair and climbed up. With her baby bump, she was not quite as agile as she used to be, so he held out his hand to help balance her as she lowered her pussy onto his cock.

Thane groaned loudly as she moved up and down on his shaft, not caring who could hear him. "God, you're hot!"

She blushed, smiling down at him.

Thane grabbed her hips, throwing his head back as his whole body tensed for a massive orgasm. There was no holding it off any longer, so he gave into his primal desire. Grunting with each thrust, he filled her with his seed.

For the first time since his awakening, he felt like a man.

Afterward, he commanded she lay beside him. Even with the passage of time, he still knew her body and soon had her moaning in pleasure. Although his movements were slow, once he found her G-spot, it didn't take a lot of stimulation to bring her to the edge.

Leaning forward to kiss her, he murmured, "Come

for me, babygirl."

Thane was gratified to feel her pussy tighten power-fully around his finger as she found release.

"I love watching you come," he said gruffy when she opened her eyes after the last pulse.

Brie stared up at him with a look of love so intense it made his heart skip a beat. He pulled her closer, giving himself a few moments to revel in this familiar intimacy before letting her go.

"Do you think you can get dressed in under a mi-nute?" he asked with a chuckle after glancing at the clock.

Her eyes sparkled as she took on his challenge. "We're about to find out!"

Brie walked into the hospital room the next day holding a small box tied with a blue bow. She smiled as she held it out to Thane.

"What's this for?"

"It's not from me. It's from Celestia. She asked me to give it to you, and wanted you to know how happy she is that you are awake and recovering."

"That is kind of her. Do you mind opening it for me, babygirl?"

"Not at all, Sir," Brie answered, moving closer. As she untied the bow and laid the blue ribbon on the tray, she told him, "Celestia said she thought of you as soon as she saw it and knew it was meant for you."

When Brie lifted the lid, she let out a small gasp. She presented it to him, murmuring, "It's so beautiful…"

Thane looked inside the box and saw a small tie pin in the shape of a violin. It appeared to be made from old watch parts. Thane took it out of the box to look at it more closely. He was impressed with the details on the miniature metal violin. "Truly exquisite and unique," he stated.

Looking at the tiny violin brought back a flood of memories.

Papa…

God, how he wished his father was here now. Thane longed to introduce Brie to him and hear his joyful laughter as he fulfilled his role as grandpa to their child—he would have made an excellent grandfather.

Thane glanced at Brie with tears in his eyes. "I miss him."

"I know, Sir," she said with empathy. "But we will continue to make him a part of our lives. Our baby will know about your father. I promise."

Thane nodded, too choked up to speak.

His child deserved to know the love that his father would have lavished on her, but it could never be. Alonzo would be relegated forever to a memory shared with their child. It wasn't enough.

"We need to take the baby to Italy."

Brie grinned, rubbing her stomach. "That's a wonderful idea. Our baby deserves to be part of your big Italian family from the very beginning, and I know it will make Nonno and Nonna so happy."

"Yes," he agreed. "We'll see to it that our child never hurts for love."

Welcome Party

"Ah, Sir Davis," Gray said in his velvety smooth voice. "I see you've mastered death as well as life."

Thane smirked at the comment, holding out his hand, genuinely glad the trainer had come for a visit. "I'm grateful to see you again, Gray." He was surprised that the instant Gray entered his room, the fog of uncertainty he'd been feeling about Durov's future began to dissipate.

Grasping Thane's hand firmly, he stated, "There was never a doubt you would return to Brianna. You are far too stubborn to give up on her. I know this for a fact."

Thane glanced at Brie. "Some things are worth fighting for."

"Agreed, which is why I came today. May I say I'm surprised I did not receive a request from you to assist with Durov."

Gray's comment caused Thane concern as Wallace's youthful face came to mind. He suddenly realized how risky the plan he was concocting truly was. People might die trying to save Durov.

"No offense, Gray, but I wouldn't accept your help even if you offered. This will be a perilous mission, and you have Celestia to care for."

"Actually, I was not offering to go. My plan was to remain here to look after...the vile flower." He said the last two words with distaste, asserting his dislike for Lilly without speaking her name aloud. "However, I know someone who has the extensive experience required for this rescue."

"What I'm proposing is dangerous, but I have no other option with time running out."

"Let every person decide what they are willing to risk," Gray advised. "All you need to do is tell us the plan, and those who volunteer will act as your hands and feet."

Thane felt a quickening in his spirit, believing for the first time that his rescue plan might have a solid chance. However, without the help of Durov's brothers, any attempt at rescue would be futile. "We won't get any-where without the support of the brothers."

"I'm confident you will attain it," Gray replied. "You are an articulate and persuasive man."

"Sir, I know you are the man who can convince them," Brie cried excitedly, the hope in her voice igniting his own.

Thane began formulating a new direction to take in his conversation with the brothers. "Once I get the ransom back on the table, we can execute the plan for the extraction."

"Let us know when you're ready to meet, and we will

gather here." Gray nodded to him, giving Brie an encouraging smile as he turned to leave.

Brie bowed her head. "Thank you for coming, Marquis."

Thane added confidently, "We'll be speaking soon."

"Good. I look forward to it."

As he was walking out, Thane spotted his uncle standing in the hallway. He turned to Brie and asked, "Could you tell him to come in, babygirl?"

His uncle walked into the room with his arm held tightly around his wife, Judy. Both were staring at Thane nervously as if they couldn't quite believe he was awake and conscious.

"Unc."

"Oh, my God," Jack cried, letting go of his wife as he rushed forward to hug Thane. "You're okay. Oh, my boy, my boy..." He grabbed Thane's face in both hands as if needing to confirm it. "You're back!"

Thane closed his eyes for a moment, soaking in his uncle's intense love while the man hugged him tight and cried on Thane's shoulder.

Judy was similarly affected, sniffling and dabbing her eyes as she smiled at him.

He could not explain why, but there was a powerful force associated with their unconditional love. His uncle's maternal connection made it even more significant, considering Ruth had abandoned him as a youth. While Thane could not understand the reasons behind it, he was nonetheless fortified by their love—and deeply grateful for it.

"We were so sorry about what happened to your

Russian friend. I felt just terrible watching the video of it," Judy told them both.

Because of Wallace and Gray's recent visits, Thane was able to answer her with conviction. "We will get him back, Auntie."

Her lip trembled when she told him, "To hear your voice again, Thane. It's like hearing the voice of an angel."

"An exaggeration, but thank you."

Brie hugged Judy, adding in her two cents. "I agree completely with you."

Judy looked down at Brie's stomach, her smile growing wider. "Every time I see you now, your baby bump gets a little bigger. Have you found out if it's a boy or girl yet?"

"No, but Sir is joining me for an ultrasound in a few days, and I can't wait to find out!"

Thane smiled to himself, certain he already knew the answer. However, he didn't want to spoil the surprise for Brie and remained quiet.

"Is there anything we can do for you, Thane? Anyone you would like us to call?" Jack asked him.

Judy suddenly turned red and glanced at Brie and then at her husband. "I don't know if that's such a good idea, honey. You know what happened the last time I was in charge of phone calls..."

Thane's curiosity was piqued. "Tell me, Auntie."

She blushed a deeper shade of red. "I'm so sorry, Thane, but I forgot to call Rytsar Durov after your accident."

Her confession brought about a flood of understanding concerning the rift between his two college friends. Thane nodded to her, relieved it was a simple mistake and not something more grievous.

"Everything worked out. Don't give it another thought," Brie assured her, giving Judy an extra squeeze.

Thane appreciated his offer. "Unc, at this point, I don't really need anything from you. But why not ask Brie?"

Jack put his arm around Brie and smiled at her. "You've helped me out countless times in the past when you worked at the tobacco shop. Is there anything I can do for you, young lady?"

She grimaced, looking almost apologetic when she answered, "Would you be willing to check on my cat and clean out the litter box?"

"Certainly," he replied without hesitation.

"You won't ever see Shadow, but he's there all alone. With me staying here at the hospital and Rytsar gone—" She broke mid-sentence but quickly collected herself. "I want to make sure he's well taken care of."

Jack gave her a quick hug. "Not a problem. Judy and I are happy to help."

Thane stared at Judy and Jack in silence, humbled by the fact he was here with them, no longer a ghost imprisoned in a paralyzed body. "You know, there was a point where I thought I would never see you two again."

Fresh tears started as Judy sucked in a sob.

"I knew you were a fighter, Thane," Jack replied. "You have been since you were a boy. It's something I've always admired about you."

"And you are my rock, Unc. You've always been

there for me, even when I was a resentful ass of a teenager. Never judging, no matter what direction my life took."

"You've always had a solid head on your shoulders, and a good heart. I couldn't be prouder of you."

Such high praise was embarrassing, but Thane nodded in appreciation.

He heard the sound of the clock beside him ticking off each second as they conversed, making him anxious. Durov was running out of time.

"While I dislike cutting this short, I—"

"Say no more," Judy insisted. "We know you need your rest." She gave him a quick kiss, and his uncle gave him one more hug before they hurried out of the room.

"I'm so glad they came to visit," Brie sighed as she shut the door behind them.

"They are good people," he agreed. "I am a lucky man."

Glancing at the anniversary clock on the counter, he smiled at Brie. "Do you know that this clock was a welcomed sound in my coma?"

"Really?" Brie's face lit up. "This is my parents' wedding gift to us. Daddy took it with him whenever he had to travel for long periods of time. He said it helped whenever he got lonely because it reminded him we would be reunited soon."

Thane held out his hand to her and pulled Brie close. "It served the same purpose for me." He didn't bother to tell her that each tick now reminded him that his friend was in mortal danger and there wasn't a second to lose.

Kissing her on the forehead, he informed Brie, "It's time I make that call to Russia."

"You aren't going to rest?" she asked in concern.

"No, babygirl, we're going to bring Durov home."

She threw her arms around him, nearly squeezing the breath out of him in her enthusiasm. "Back home to us."

"While I speak to his brothers, can you call my lawyer, Thompson, to let him know he needs to pencil in a few hours for me? It's do or die time."

Thane thought on that for a moment and shook his head. Dying wasn't an option—for any of them.

After securing the allegiance and support of Andrev, the last brother Thane thought would ever champion Durov's rescue, he was forced to take a moment to actually rest—Nurse Abby threatened to sedate him if he did not.

Brie lay in his arms while he stroked her hair and he forced himself to relax. Thane made it a point to keep his eyes open, refusing to shut them for extended periods after having spent far too much time in the dark.

Brie lifted her head suddenly, startled by a commotion just outside the door.

The door burst open and a huge bouquet marched into the room, carried by a tiny deliveryman. Following the flowers, another man holding a huge white box walked in. Behind him was Anderson himself, hefting an old-fashioned boom box on his shoulder with the song

"Best Day of My Life" by American Authors blaring loudly.

The man with the bouquet tried to hand the giant vase to Brie, but Anderson stopped him. "No, no. You go put that on the counter over there. This little mama can't be lifting heavy things in her delicate state."

The man apologized and placed the large bouquet down where Anderson had indicated.

"What's this?" Brie cried out in awe, ogling the giant flower bouquet.

"What did you say, young Brie?" Anderson asked, turning down the music slightly.

"I hate to tell you this," she giggled, "but it's not my birthday today."

"Of course it isn't," he replied, flashing her a charming smile.

Brie grinned, shrugging her shoulders. "So what's the meaning of this massive flower creation?"

"You do not know this, but the day I had my car accident, I had a bouquet exactly like this strapped in the truck. I was coming to deliver it to you when the old lady and that dang turtle changed my plans. Since the original never made it to its final destination, I asked my florist to make another."

Brie began stroking the various blossoms, taking in the scent of each flower as she explored the unusual arrangement with her fingers. "Master Anderson, this is like a work of art."

"You like it, then?"

"I love it, and am thoroughly entranced by it."

"What has you sending my wife such an impressive

display?" Thane asked with a smirk.

Anderson's answer was honest and true to his nature. "I just wanted to see young Brie smile again. She's been through too much lately. You both have."

Anderson pointed to the counter, instructing the man holding the large box to place it beside the flowers. Handing the deliverymen each a wad of bills and giving a hearty handshake, he sent them on their way. Thane did not miss the mischievous glint in Anderson's eyes when he closed the door behind them.

"And now for the real reason I came…"

Brie tilted her head, giggling. "What are you up to, Master Anderson?"

"Open the box and find out."

When she started to lift the lid, he stopped her. "Wait! Before you do, why don't you tell me what you *think* it is?"

She stared at the large pastry box with an amused expression. "It's really big for a baked good, but I still have to go with a cake."

"Good guess, young Brie."

Anderson gave Thane a wink.

Brie stood on tiptoes to look inside after she lifted the lid, and let out a pleased squeal. "It's so pretty with all those flowers! What flavor is it?"

Brad put his hand to his ear, "What?"

Brie turned around to face him and asked in a louder voice, speaking over the music, "What kind of cake?"

He turned off the music completely and said nothing, grinning from ear to ear.

Brie's eyes suddenly grew wide and she turned back

to the box staring, transfixed, at it. Leaning forward while turning her head slightly, Brie appeared to be listening to the cake.

"Master Anderson, are those…?"

"They are, young Brie."

He looked at Thane and chuckled. "I brought your wife a pussy cake."

Anderson walked over to Brie and freed the intricately decorated cake from its box, setting the cake on the floor.

"How many do you think there are?" he asked her.

"I have no idea," Brie squeaked, pressing her hands to her chest in excitement. "But their little mews are so stinking cute!"

Thane stared at Anderson and raised an eyebrow. "Kittens?"

"I had to bring the music to drown out the noises coming from the box. I wouldn't want you to get in trouble."

"I'm not the one who's going to get in trouble," Thane stated, looking back at the cake. He found himself captivated by the smile on Brie's face as Anderson unscrewed the top of the plastic confection. The minute he lifted it off, a passel of kittens tumbled out.

"Oh, my goodness!" Brie cried, picking up one and then another, trying to pile all the furry creatures on her lap.

Anderson grinned at Thane. "I knew the kittens would be just what the doctor ordered. However, I wasn't sure the hospital staff would agree. Hence the party theme to distract the staff from my true intentions."

"Aren't they the cutest, Sir?" Brie cooed, covered in kittens crawling all over her.

Anderson picked up a calico and walked over to Thane, placing the tiny animal on his chest. "She's my favorite. Saucy little spirit, but a sweetie just like Cayenne."

Even though he was not an animal person, Thane couldn't deny those big eyes, and that tiny pink nose with long whiskers was appealing, especially when the kitten rubbed its furry head against his chin. The creature didn't care that he was an invalid. It didn't know that terrible things were happening—it was simply a bundle of carefree innocence.

Brie giggled from the floor. "I can't believe you have so many black kittens, Master Anderson."

"I know…" Anderson huffed in irritation. "If you can believe it, all the black ones are male. It's as if the black bastard is taunting me with his offspring."

Brie broke out in a fit of laughter.

One of the kittens was frightened by her sudden outburst and ran to Anderson, trying to climb up his pants leg. He picked up the tiny black ball of fur and lifted it to his face. "Even though the last thing I ever wanted were kittens, I have to admit they are a kick to have around. And this one?" He turned it around so they could see its face. "I've been told this guy is extremely rare—black like his father, with blue eyes like his mother."

"Too adorable!" Brie agreed.

Thane shook his head, surprised that Anderson

seemed to be handling the whole Cayenne/Shadow debacle exceedingly well. "So, what do you plan to do with them?"

Anderson cradled the little kitten against his muscular chest. "I'm not sure yet. There's no way I can keep all six, but I can't stomach the idea of giving any of them away."

"Really?"

He coughed self-consciously. "Yeah, the little buggers have started to grow on me."

"I always suspected that deep inside that baby-hating man lived a giant softie." Brie grinned as she rubbed her round belly, glancing at him teasingly. "I bet you are going to make an exceptional pseudo-uncle for our little one." As soon as she said it, the expression on her face changed, and she bit her lip, trying to keep her tears at bay.

Thane knew she was thinking of Durov.

Suddenly, a vision of his friend beaten and bloody came to Thane's mind. It felt like he'd been gut-punched, and he struggled to breathe.

The kitten on his chest moved closer, putting its paws on his chin and leaning forward to lick his nose.

Brie burst out in giggles, shaking off her melancholy. "That's so adorable!"

Thane picked the kitten up in both hands and shook his head. "You don't know this yet, but you have to ask permission before you can lick me."

Anderson's low laughter joined Brie's lyrical one.

Thane glanced over at Brie, grateful for Anderson's willingness to bend the rules that granted them this unexpected and welcomed distraction.

When he set the kitten back down on his chest, it started purring as it kneaded him with its tiny claws. Thane frowned and was about to pick it back up when Anderson commanded, "Just give it a sec."

Sure enough, moments later, the kitten stopped and lay down, curling into a small ball on his chest, still purring loudly.

"She must like you, buddy," Anderson stated. "If you really want her, I'll make the sacrifice."

As endearing as the kitten was, Thane did not want to take on the responsibility. "I wouldn't dream of splitting up your feline family."

Anderson smirked. "I won't be offering again, no matter how much you beg."

"Truthfully, Master Anderson, it wouldn't be fair to Shadow," Brie told him. "A father should be with all of his children, not just one."

His low laughter was ripe with sarcasm. "Yeah, that'll be the day."

Brie got a funny expression on her face. Giving each kitten a kiss before she set them on the floor, Brie walked over to Thane and leaned over, cupping her hand to whisper her idea in his ear.

"Okay, what are you up to, young Brie?" Brad demanded.

Brie smiled sweetly. "Do you remember that bet you made with me at the apartment?"

He looked confused for a second, before his eyes sparked in remembrance. "I do, now that you mention it."

"You bet on Sir's first words when he woke up. But, sadly, Master Anderson, you were wrong."

Anderson shrugged, grinning at Thane. "Hey, I was certain your first words would be directed at me. What can I say?"

Thane shook his head in amusement.

Brie explained to Thane, "At the time, I told Master Anderson I knew exactly what I was going to buy with the winnings, but I've changed my mind."

"Woman's prerogative," Anderson replied amiably.

She walked back to play with the kittens, smiling at him mischievously as she passed by.

Anderson turned to Thane. "So, what is she planning?"

Thane didn't crack a smile when he said, "Brie mentioned that Shadow takes his responsibility to the kittens very seriously."

"Wait," Anderson said, holding his hand up. "*Please* don't tell me young Brie plans to write another love story about cats."

Brie snorted in amusement. "Can you seriously tell me that you didn't feel the love when you read their passionate romance?"

"I most definitely did not."

Brie arched her eyebrow. "So if I read that story to you right now, there would be absolutely no response—at all?" Her eyes drifted down to his crotch.

Anderson covered up his groin, hiding it from her scrutiny. "I make no such claims, but it wouldn't be because of the story, darlin'."

Brie giggled.

"Please tell me it's not another story," he begged Thane.

"Fine," he answered. "It's not another story."

"Good," he replied, sounding relieved. A few seconds later, however, he frowned at Thane. "Did you just say that because I told you to?"

Thane smiled.

"Young Brie…" Anderson implored.

She gave him an innocent look. "What?"

"No more stories from you."

"Oh, don't worry. This isn't coming from me."

"What isn't?"

Brie picked up two of the black kittens, giving them each an Eskimo kiss, ignoring the question.

Anderson looked back to Thane.

Thane nodded his head toward Brie and watched her for several moments, touched to see the open joy on her face. He glanced back at Anderson in gratefulness.

Anderson understood, and tipped an imaginary hat. "Anytime, buddy."

A few days later, Thane was looking at Durov's rescue team: Wallace, the boy he had trained to collar Brie; Captain, a friend of Gallant's who'd become like family after the airplane crash; and Samantha, a long-time friend and colleague, who shared a complicated past with Durov.

Anderson, Baron, Gray, and Boa were also in attendance, having all agreed to assist in the dangerous mission. However, Thane had quickly whittled it down to these few because of the extreme risks involved.

He felt the three he'd chosen stood the best chance of getting Durov back with minimum peril. There was no point to saving his Russian brother, only to lose someone else he cared about in the process.

Thane grabbed the rails of his bed and forced himself into an upright position. He looked at each person there, inspired by their bravery. "Thank you for your friendship, your courage, and your selfless hearts. Each one of you here has offered the same sacrifice, and for that I am eternally grateful..." His voice faltered, and he lay back down, tears of gratitude blurring his vision.

He would never forget this moment or the people standing before him.

Captain took over the meeting, being a trained leader who understood the urgency of the mission ahead. "We need nonessentials to leave so we can go over the plan in order to execute it quickly and efficiently."

The four men staying behind shook hands with those who were leaving for Russia, wishing them good luck and a quick return. It was sobering for Thane to realize, as they all shook hands, that there was a distinct possibility one or more of them might not make it back.

By the end of the night, each person knew their role and how the mission would play out. While Vlad would act as the spokesperson for the family and deal with the Koslovs while negotiating the ransom, Andrev would join the team and assist where he could.

Having extensively researched the Koslov brothers,

and knowing their unbalanced nature, Thane determined that Samantha should act as the leader during the ransom exchange, with Andrev remaining out of sight. Thane was afraid that having one of the Durovs physically present would take away from the impersonal nature of the business, adding a dynamic that could complicate things.

The only catch was getting the Koslovs to agree to having a third-party act as a representative for the family. He would have to rely on Vlad and Andrev to convince them.

Gavriil was known to have a fetish for subduing and punishing strong women, but Samantha was a skilled Domme, and he felt confident she could exploit that to her advantage. Having Captain and Wallace take on subservient roles would make them appear as less of a threat during the potentially volatile exchange.

"You are not to engage," Thane stated emphatically. "Make it a quick exchange and get Durov the hell out of there. These men are infamous for changing their minds at the flip of a dime and won't hesitate to kill you if they get spooked."

"Understood," Captain replied. "The helicopter will be prepped and ready for takeoff as soon as we have him in our possession."

Thane appreciated the military background Captain brought to this operation. With Samantha's command of the Russian language, as well as her quick wit, Thane felt certain she would be able to navigate any unexpected issues that arose during the exchange. As for Wallace, his youth and strength could prove vital if things suddenly went south.

Before the team left, Thane told them, "Durov's life is not worth one of yours. If it comes to that, leave him behind. Anton would not want you to sacrifice your life for his, and neither would I. You three must come back alive, with or without Durov."

He saw Samantha balk at his statement and met her gaze. "Do you understand?"

She nodded, but tears filled her eyes.

Thane shook hands with each of them. He wished, with all his heart, that it were he and not them taking this risk for his brother.

To be left behind was almost more than he could bear.

Brie cried as she hugged each person, thanking them through her tears.

When they were alone again in the hospital room, he was overwhelmed with the weight of responsibility he felt for those three, but it was quickly followed by a hope that settled over him like a blanket of protection.

Thane pulled Brie close and kissed her tear-stained cheek, stating confidently, "They will bring him home."

Lucinda

The silence had been deafening, but necessary, as Thane waited to hear from the rescue party. They had been instructed not to break their silence until all of them were safely out from behind enemy lines.

Thane stared continuously at his phone the day the ransom exchange was scheduled to take place. He and Brie were anxious for it to ring even though they knew there was a possibility the news might be devastating.

There had been several occasions over the course of many weeks when he'd lost that internal connection he'd always felt with Durov. At this point, he could not rely on it, because he refused to accept any other reality than that his brother was alive and returning home.

When the phone finally rang and an unfamiliar Russian number popped up on the screen, Thane felt a moment of panic, afraid of what he would learn. But he picked up the phone to answer it, looking at Brie with confidence he did not feel.

He answered in formal Russian, unsure who was on the other end, "*Zdravstvuy?*"

Durov's rich voice filled his ear. "Brother!"

Thane momentarily lost the power of speech. He had not anticipated how deeply hearing his friend's familiar voice would affect him.

"Durov, is that really you?"

Brie cried out, "Is that Rytsar, Sir?"

"It is I, brother," Durov confirmed.

Thane's voice faltered, his tone gravelly as he fought to speak through his many emotions. "Oh, hell... I cannot tell you how good it is to hear your voice again."

"I feel the same, comrade."

"Where are you now?"

Brie burst out in excitement, "He's alive. Oh, my God. Rytsar's alive!"

Thane's elation was cut short when Durov said, "Wallace has been injured. We are headed to my physician even as we speak."

"How bad is he?"

"It is bad, *moy droog*, but...he will live."

"Thank God. And you?"

"I will recover, as well."

Thane tried to relay the news to Brie but she was so thrilled, she grabbed the phone and cried, "Come home to us!"

She handed the phone back to him, tears of happiness running down her face.

Thane told Durov, "I would be there if I could."

"And I would have kicked your ass if you had come. You have Brie and the babe to look after."

Thane chuckled, but he could not shake the helplessness he felt. "What do you need me to do?"

"Nothing more, comrade. You have orchestrated a miracle. One I never imagined was possible."

Thane and Brie were forced to wait for a reunion with him because Durov insisted on remaining there. "What they have done to Wallace was gratuitous and cruel. The Koslov organization is no longer stable, brother. Even among the unlawful, there is a set code of conduct. They must be stopped."

Durov was determined to take out the Koslov brothers, and both Captain and Samantha were staying in Russia to assist him. Wallace, on the other hand, was returning due to the serious injury he'd sustained.

The only information Thane had was that Wallace was stable and able to travel. Thane bore the responsibility of his fate, having knowingly put him in a situation that was dangerous.

Brie cried when Wallace walked through the door with a sterile gauze bandage covering his left eye. Thane felt a lump in his throat as he greeted the man.

The loss of an eye should have been his to bear, not Wallace's.

"Tell us what happened."

Wallace's voice was calm as he stated matter-of-factly, "Durov is safe. We all made it out alive. He would have died that day if we hadn't shown up."

"Oh, my God!" Brie cried, covering her mouth.

"The Koslovs are as crazy as you said they were," he

told Thane. "Someone had to sacrifice, and I knew it needed to be me."

"Why you?"

"They would have taken Captain's eye or killed us all. The decision was clear."

Thane looked at him with both admiration and remorse.

"Sir Davis, I knew two things when I went to Russia—that something significant was going to happen, and I was meant to be there."

"It should have been me."

Wallace snorted, laughing lightly. "You don't know how many times I've said that same thing in my own life. But I don't feel that way anymore." He seemed almost surprised by it, and shook his head. "Wow...between my recent visit to Trevor's grave and Durov's rescue, I am free of that guilt." He looked at Brie in wonder. "I am free."

She wrapped her arms around him, smiling through her tears as she embraced him. "I'm glad."

It would have been an odd response for a man who had just lost his eye if they hadn't understood his history and the significance of this moment.

Thane shook Wallace's hand. "I owe you my gratitude, and you have my utmost respect. You are no longer the young man who came to The Center looking for meaning in your life. It is a rare person who can free themselves from a difficult past, but the potential once they do is limitless."

"That's exactly how I feel, and I can't begin to tell you how incredible it is."

"Is there anything we can do? Anyway we can help you, Faelan?" Brie asked.

"Just treat me like you normally would." Wallace pointed to his face. "I don't want or need your sympathy." He glanced at Davis. "I'm certain you understand where I'm coming from."

"I do," Thane agreed, "but I also know from experience that you will have low moments. We are here when you need us."

"I'll keep that in mind."

Thane was hit with an overwhelming feeling of gratitude and struggled to speak. "Wallace, thank you for saving him."

He nodded. "Family."

Thane received a letter from Lucinda a few days later. He pulled the folded note out of the envelope and opened it up. The handwriting was in large, child-like print with rainbows drawn all around the borders.

Mr. Davis,
You are my hero.
Can I come see you?
Love, Lucinda

He would have preferred to wait until he was fully recovered, not wanting the child to see him as the invalid he was now. However, Thane was unsure how long recovery would take and didn't feel it was fair to make her wait because of his pride.

There was another element to it. Although he had been told the little girl was doing well since the crash, he needed to have that personal contact to confirm it for himself. Those last seconds together had haunted his dreams every night since he'd awakened from the coma.

Thane had been disturbed to learn that the stewardess, Viola, who had helped the young girl before takeoff, had not been among the survivors. In order to bring closure for everyone, Thane wanted to invite the family of the young woman to join their private reunion.

Picking up the phone, he made a call to Lucinda.

"Hello, this is Thane Davis. I would like to speak to Miss Jefferys."

"Oh, Mr. Davis, it is such an honor to hear from you," Dorothy, her mother, gushed. "Let me get my daughter for you."

There was excited chatter in the background, and then he heard the girl's shy voice.

"Hello?"

"Miss Jefferys?"

She giggled. "Yes."

"This is Thane Davis. I just received your letter."

"You did?"

"Yes, and I would like it if you and your mother would come for a visit."

"Yay!" she cried happily.

He heard Lucinda tell her mother. "He said yes, Mommy!"

The little girl told Thane, "I have a picture I made. I

saved it for you."

"I look forward to seeing it. Can you put your mother back on the phone? I would like to talk to her."

"Okay. See you soon!"

Thane explained to Dorothy his wish to include Viola's family. "I feel it will help them reconcile her loss by meeting the young lady she assisted."

"Of course. We owe her for sitting Lucinda next to you so, by all means, invite them to join us."

"Excellent. I want to assure you that there will be no press allowed in the room, and I have arranged for you and your daughter to be escorted to and from the hospital. Your privacy and well-being are important to me."

"Thank you, Mr. Davis," she said. "I deeply appreciate that."

"I will speak to Viola's family and make the arrangements, then."

After he finished with the call, Brie voiced a concern she had. "Sir, you can't know the outpouring of support and prayers you received from the entire community. While I agree that no one should be present for Lucinda's visit, would it be possible to give a statement to the press afterward?"

"I do not want Lucinda or either family to feel uncomfortable by fielding questions. That is not what this is about."

"I completely agree, but what if you were the only one to speak? You wouldn't have to take any questions, either. Only offer to give them a general statement."

Thane thought about it for a moment. "It would allow me to preserve the personal aspect of this gathering while acknowledging the help we've received."

"Yes, that sounds perfect. You may not believe this, but I think the community needs closure as well, Sir."

He nodded to her. "Frankly, I cannot fathom the extent of the community's involvement in my recovery, but I'm sincerely grateful for it."

Brie pulled out the huge album she'd created that included every newspaper clipping, card sent, and email message received which she had printed out. "This is the reason I believe it is necessary."

Thane flipped through the album, scanning each page. He found himself stopping at notes written by children, and the cursive penmanship of older citizens. He was thoroughly overwhelmed by the outpouring of sympathy and well wishes found between the pages.

He closed the book, waiting a few seconds as he took it all in. "I agree with you. It's important I thank everyone for their concern and prayers."

Brie took his hand and placed it against her cheek. "I was not alone in helping with your recovery. There was a whole city behind you."

"You weren't alone, but…" He grasped the back of her neck and pulled her to him, kissing her deeply. "…you were the only one with me every moment."

"I love you, Sir, and couldn't bear a life without you."

He crushed her against his chest, grateful for this second chance he'd been given. His suspended time in his pseudo Hell had changed him. The emotional barriers he'd constructed to protect himself had no place in his new life.

Life was too short to live behind walls.

Extra security was put in place as Lucinda, her mother, and Viola's parents and siblings, gathered together in a large room located in the center of the hospital.

Thane had asked Brie to shave him before helping him to dress in a white button-down shirt with a tie. Although he was still gaunt and bed-ridden, he wanted, as much as possible, to look like himself for Lucinda.

Viola's family was the first to arrive. Thane had wanted to speak with them alone before they met Lucinda. He understood there would be justifiable tears when he talked about the crash and wanted to spare the little girl from any discomfort that might cause.

"I'm grateful to meet you all," Thane told them when the family of five entered the room.

"It is good to meet someone who knew Viola, and was one of the last to see her," Mr. Horne told him somberly. "It has been difficult for us these past few months."

"We still can't accept she's really gone," Mrs. Horne said with pain in her eyes.

"That's why I asked you to come. We're here to mourn her loss together and celebrate Viola's good heart."

Mrs. Horne stared at him, asking with a hint of anguish in her voice, "You said you would tell us about my daughter's last moments?"

"I'll tell you everything I remember. But before I begin, I want you to know that although Viola and I were only acquaintances, she stood out as an exceptional young woman and was well respected among our circle of friends." Thane was unsure if her family knew about Viola's BDSM lifestyle, so he kept the details general.

When Mrs. Horne started crying, her older daughter grabbed her hand, both women letting the tears fall as they waited for Thane to speak.

One of the young men told him, "Please, go on."

Thane nodded. "I was unaware that Viola was on the plane until she seated Lucinda next to me." He looked at Viola's father with sympathy. "That decision saved Lucinda's life."

Thane turned his attention to the mother and sister. "Viola was especially attentive to the child and seemed happy that morning. As for me, it was an unexpected pleasure that she was on my flight to Dubai."

Thane shook his head, remembering those last frightening moments as the plane went down. "Being a professional, Viola expected a successful emergency landing, as I did.

"I can assure you that the end came quickly. I trust her experience those last few seconds was similar to mine—a calmness that settled over her, followed by acceptance before she blacked out. There would have been minimal suffering, if any."

Mrs. Horne let out a gasp before she started sobbing on her daughter's shoulder.

The father nodded his head slowly, taking in Thane's

words.

Thane focused his attention on the two brothers. "She often shared with her friends the pranks you played on each other."

The two men chuckled sadly, holding in emotions that had yet to see release. It was hard to see the devastation in each of their faces, knowing nothing would ever be the same for this family.

"I am deeply grieved that she did not survive. Viola was an admirable young woman with a lifetime ahead of her."

Her mother nodded her head vigorously, trying to stifle her sobs in a handkerchief her husband had given her.

"I'm certain Viola would take great comfort in knowing that she had a hand in saving Lucinda's life. She lives on through the child. I hope you can find solace in that."

Mrs. Horne sighed deeply as she dried her tears, blowing into the handkerchief several times before speaking. "We do, Mr. Davis. Just as we take comfort in your survival. It is as you say. Part of Viola lives on in both your lives."

"She does," he affirmed. "And it means a lot to meet you today, even though the circumstances are tragic."

"Part of me died that day," she admitted.

Brie spoke up, her voice quavering. "I understand, Mrs. Horne, and I am so very sorry for your loss."

The mother only nodded, but Viola's sister walked over to Brie and gave her a hug. Lightening the heavy moment, she asked, "When is your baby due?"

Brie looked down at her bulging stomach. "We have

three more months."

"I'm glad your child will have a father," Mr. Horne stated, glancing at Thane.

"Yes, that makes me happy, as well," the mother agreed, smiling through her tears.

"As you may already know," Thane explained, "Lucinda walked away from the plane crash with only a broken arm. She does not remember the crash itself and, since the accident, her mother and father are reconciling. I was told he is looking at moving back to the States."

"That seems promising," Viola's sister said. Her voice sounded so similar to Viola's that Thane felt a momentary twinge of pain.

Thankfully, Lucinda and her mother arrived, providing the youthful exuberance they all needed.

Lucinda walked in with a huge smile on her face, swinging the picture she'd made in her hand, but as soon as she spotted Thane, she stopped, grabbed her mother's hand, and hid behind her.

Brie whispered to Thane, "She was shy with me, too, in the beginning." Thane turned his attention on Dorothy so the child wouldn't feel pressured and held out his hand to shake hers.

Dorothy moved over to him, ignoring his outstretched hand, choosing to hug him, instead. "Mr. Davis, how can I ever thank you?"

Thane was surprised by the hug but handled it in stride, looking past her at Lucinda to give the little girl a wink.

"I did nothing more than any other person would," he assured Dorothy.

She laughed softly, shaking her head. "Most men would demand another seat if a child sat next to them—especially on such a long flight."

Thane gestured to Brie. "As you can see, we will soon be in the family way. I was honored to have Miss Jefferys as a seatmate."

Lucinda peeked her head out, responding to his formal title for her.

Thane glanced at Viola's family and remembered something. He asked Dorothy, "Does Miss Jefferys still have the airplane pin that the stewardess gave to her?"

"I do!" Lucinda cried out, grinning. "Mommy put it in a special case so it won't get lost. She says it's my lucky pin."

Thane could see that Mrs. Horne was holding back her tears as the entire family smiled at the little girl.

When Brie noticed the child staring nervously at the five strangers, she stepped in. "Lucinda, did you know the nice lady who gave you that pin was named Viola? Her mommy came to say hi to you, and so did her daddy, sister, and two brothers."

Lucinda stared at the five of them but didn't make a peep.

Brie added with a giggle, "I heard that Viola's brothers liked to do silly things to make her laugh."

Lucinda broke into a smile and waved shyly at the two young men.

The entire family waved back, the lightness in their expressions letting Thane know that this arranged meeting was proving beneficial.

Lucinda finally turned to face Thane, looking up at

him from the edge of the bed.

He glanced at the paper in her hand and asked, "Is that the picture?"

Her shyness seemed to melt away as she held the picture out to show him and said proudly, "I made this."

The drawing was of one tiny stick figure with yellow curls and one bigger one with a straight line of brown on top of the head. There was a giant rainbow above them.

Thane tried to keep his emotions at bay, remembering those last seconds when he covered her with his body as the plane went down.

"That looks just like us."

She thrust out the paper to him. "It's for you."

Thane took it from her and looked the drawing over, appreciating the miracle of this picture and the fact they had both survived. "I will put it in a frame and hang it up in my house."

"Good," she answered. "I got a pink cast. What did you get?"

Thane gave her a sad look. "I didn't get a pink cast."

"I'm sorry."

"I don't mind because I got this pretty picture instead."

Lucinda broke out in delightful giggles that filled the room, providing the healing salve all of their hearts needed.

Afterward, Thane was wheeled back to his hospital

room. Once he was ready to give his statement, reporters from various news outlets were invited in. Once the cameras and sound equipment were in place, the lights were turned on. Thane was suddenly blinded, and felt the heat of the lamps on his face.

He nodded that he was prepared to give his statement and gestured Brie over to him, holding her hand.

"I want to take this moment to thank every person who has reached out to me through letters, emails, positive thoughts, and prayers. I fully believe your compassion made a difference in my recovery. But it wasn't just me that you helped." Thane kissed Brie's hand before continuing. "Your support meant the world to my wife, making a difficult time easier for her. I thank you for that."

He looked directly into the lens of the middle camera. "When tragedy strikes, that's when the real heroes make themselves known. To all of you out there, we give you our sincerest thanks."

Brie bowed her head slightly and smiled at the camera. "Thank you, everyone."

After the lights were turned off, Thane turned Brie's head and kissed her on the lips. "I love you."

Unbeknownst to him, one of the cameramen was still recording and caught the moment. Although Thane's formal statement was played on all the local networks that night, it was that intimate moment afterward that the internet grabbed onto and replayed.

Thane shook his head when Brie showed him the next day. "Remind me to never make a statement again."

Brie reviewed the ten-second short and smiled. "You

know, I will never get tired of seeing you kiss me and tell me you love me."

"You don't have to watch it, babygirl. I'm right here." He grasped her throat and kissed her deeply, enjoying the sound of her stifled moans against his lips.

Romancing Her

The elation Thane felt knowing that Durov was safe needed release, and there was no better place to do that than in Brie's arms.

"Babygirl, I would like you to dress up for me tonight," he mentioned causally as if it were an afterthought.

Brie smiled at his suggestion. "Would you like me to look fancy or sexy?"

"Dress however you feel inspired, my dear."

Brie blushed, looking at him bashfully. "It's been a long time since I've dolled myself up."

"Far too long."

Her eyes sparkled as she considered what to wear. "Oh, the possibilities…"

"Why don't you go now? You can even buy a new outfit, if you like, and meet me back here at…" Thane looked at the clock, pretending to think about it. "How about seven?"

"Would you like me to bring dinner, too?"

"No, babygirl. I just want you."

She leaned down and kissed him on the lips, grinning as she did so. "That's all I want, too, Sir."

As she was leaving, Thane commanded in a low, sultry voice, "Bring the Magic Wand."

Brie turned around to face him, biting her lip. "Oh, my…" she purred. "You've just made me all tingly inside."

Thane was hungry to take on the role as her Dominant again. Although he was limited by his physical condition, it did not affect his desire for that power exchange. The expression on her face as she left out the door let him know how much she longed for it as well.

While some Dominants relied on their skills with particular tools, he'd always relied on the mental and emotional aspects of Domination. It was fortunate, considering his physical limitations now.

Nurse Abby knocked on the door to let him know she was there before walking in. She had a large canvas bag with her. "I made sure to wait until she was gone."

"I appreciate your assistance with this on your day off."

Abby set down her bag on a chair and smiled. "I've admired your heroism from the moment you were put into my care." He was about to protest, but she put up her hand. "Little Lucinda and I are entitled to our opinions, Mr. Davis."

He chuckled.

"I have also watched your wife all these months and consider her a hero in her own right. The love and devotion she's shown through all this has been truly inspiring to me. I think highly of you both, and…" Her cheeks suddenly colored with a pink hue. "I feel honored that you asked me to help."

"You are a kind person."

She laughed self-consciously, charming in her humbleness. "Would you like me to show you what I bought with your credit card? You can let me know where you want me to set them in the room."

"By all means."

Reaching into the bag, she pulled out a glass jar. "Since candles aren't allowed, I thought some fragrant potpourri would be nice when added with this…" She pulled out a box and opened it, lifting out a black platform that had a glass pyramid on top. She inserted several batteries into the bottom of the base, then turned on the switch.

Warm orange and yellow holographic flames flickered and danced on the base.

"It will give you the romantic glow of candlelight…"

He held out his hand, fascinated by the device. "May I see it?"

Abby handed it to him.

Thane stared at it, transfixed. "Isn't it amazing what we can do with technology these days?"

"I'm so glad you like it, Mr. Davis. Where would you like me to put it?"

"Place it on the tray, along with your aromatic jar. Did you remember to get the speakers, as well?"

"Of course," she answered, taking the set out of the bag, along with a tube of lubricant.

Thane smirked, not one bit ashamed to take the lubricant from her hand. He tucked it under his pillow and asked her to place the speakers on the tray.

Abby arranged them behind the hologram on either side, and then asked for his cell phone. Connecting the phone to the speakers, she set it down on the tray and smiled. "I call it 'Romance on a Tray'."

"I quite agree."

"I also have your suit hanging in the employee lounge. Would you like me to get it and dress you?"

"Yes, thank you. I want to look presentable when I seduce my wife, and this…" he picked at the thin material of his hospital gown, "…simply won't do."

She grinned. "Let me get that suit for you, then, Mr. Davis."

Abby quickly returned with his suit and began the task of dressing him. She was efficient and professional, but the gentleness with which she handled him spoke to the care she put into her duties as a nurse.

"You are an exceptionally kindhearted woman," he told her while she worked.

Abby laughed quietly.

He gently took hold of her wrist and stopped her. "The compliment is sincere."

She blushed a deep shade of red. "Oh, Mr. Davis, I—"

"Nurse Abby, you should know the care you put into your patients helps speed their recovery."

"I just love helping people," she replied, shrugging her shoulders. "It's what I was born to do."

"That's evident in the tone of your voice, and the care you put into your duties. As a man who has experienced your nursing skills firsthand, I must thank you."

She fanned her face. "Oh, you are making me blush so hard right now."

"My intention is to express my sincerest gratitude."

"Oh, it's been expressed, and then some. Now, let me finish here." She giggled as she buttoned the two remaining buttons on his shirt. "I think that about does it," she stated when she was done. "And the flowers should be here any—"

The knock on the door alerted him to their arrival, the last item on his list.

Abby went to open the door and invited the deliveryman with a large vase of red roses to come in.

"Where would you like these, sir?"

Thane nodded toward Abby. "Let her decide. She knows where they can go so they won't block the equipment in the room."

"Good, because there are eleven more of these coming," the man told him, turning to Abby. "Miss, where should this one go?"

She pointed to the counter next to the sink and followed him out to help him bring in the others. By the time the two were done, the room was filled with the sweet scent of roses with the bouquets spread throughout the room.

After Thane had tipped the man, he told Abby, "Once our evening is over, I would like you to make sure that each nurse gets a bouquet, including yourself."

"I would be happy to, Mr. Davis." She looked around the room counting silently and lamented, "But there won't be any left for your wife if I do."

"That won't be an issue," he assured her. Thane had

already ordered a unique arrangement to be delivered to their apartment while Brie was with him tonight. A special bouquet to remind her of this first scene together as Master and sub since the plane crash.

"Is there anything more I can do?"

"Two things, actually. Would you take one of the roses and lay in on the tray, and then turn off the lights so I can see the overall effect?"

She wheeled the tray over to him so he could to reach the items on it and pulled a large blossom out of one of the vases, setting it next to the holographic flame.

Abby then reached for the switch on her way out, shutting it off. The light from the holographic fire filled the room with a warm, flickering glow.

"Perfect," he stated. When she went to turn the lights back on, he stopped her. "No, keep it like this."

"Enjoy your evening, Mr. Davis. You two deserve a night of celebration."

Thane turned on the playlist he'd selected for Brie and waited patiently for her to walk through the door. He was extremely curious about what she would be wearing.

The girl teased him by arriving in the same tailored black trench coat she'd worn during her Submissive Training days.

When Brie walked through the door, she immediately stopped. The low, erotic beat of the music added to the seductive ambiance, and he watched in satisfaction as she looked around the room in awe.

"Oh, Sir…"

Shutting the door behind her, Brie walk over to him, her eyes drawn to the dancing holographic flames. She seemed entranced by it.

"This is so amazing," she said in wonder as she looked around the room.

"Nurse Abby helped."

"She's an incredible person."

"She is…" Thane agreed. He reached out and pulled on the belt of her coat. "So, Mrs. Davis, what do you have on under this coat you're wearing?"

Brie gave him a flirtatious grin as she twisted back and forth where she stood. "I decided not to go fancy, Sir."

He growled huskily. "Show me."

Brie undid her belt and undid each button slowly, glancing at him with a shy smile that was beguiling. Opening up her coat, she revealed that she was only wearing thigh-high stockings and heels.

"You always said I looked good in these."

"Yes, you do, babygirl. Lose the coat and turn for me."

Brie set the coat over the back of a chair and then proudly stood before him, turning so he could admire every angle of her body.

"It's still true. I prefer you in nothing but stockings and heels."

She moved over to him, her ample breasts highlighted by the dancing light of the red and orange flames. Thane caressed the rounded swell of her breast, his cock already aching from seeing her naked body.

"I need you, woman."

Brie leaned closer, whispering provocatively, "Good. I need to be needed."

Thane groaned when their lips met, and he hungrily explored her mouth with his tongue. Using his senses, he took in all of Brie—reveling in her scent, the sounds of her moans, her soft skin, and the taste of those sexy lips.

He longed to take her, but chose not to give into that desire. But, oh, how he wanted to sink his cock deep into her...

Between kisses, Thane asked, "Did you bring the wand?"

She smiled, kissing him again before answering. "I did, Sir."

"Go get it."

Brie reluctantly broke away to dig through her large purse, producing the item he'd requested.

"Clean off the instrument before you plug it in and hand it to me, téa." He emphasized her sub name, officially announcing the beginning of the scene he had planned.

"It would be my pleasure, Master," she answered, bowing gracefully.

Brie was seductively slow in her movements as she performed the task, handing him the Magic Wand with a playful smile when she was done. Kneeling in an open position before him, she waited for her next task.

"Stand and undress me," Thane commanded in a low, gravelly tone.

Brie's eyes sparkled with anticipation as she obeyed,

sliding the railing down so she could complete his wishes. Just as before, she remained slow and seductive in her movements as she removed each piece of clothing, leaving him lying there naked with a raging hard-on by the time she was finished.

"Oh, Master…" she purred, gazing at his manhood hungrily.

Thane pushed himself over to the side of the bed and petted the empty space. "Join me."

She climbed onto the bed and curled up beside him, spooning her body against him.

"Open those legs, téa." Reaching down, he stroked her smooth mound, groaning when he felt how wet she was. "So wet, babygirl," he growled lustfully.

"Your princely cock has that effect on me."

Thane liked her answer and leaned forward, biting her gently on the neck as he began to play with her clit.

Brie instinctively pressed against him, her body needing the connection as much as he did.

Knowing where they were headed, and impatient to get there, Thane picked up the wand and turned it on. Brie let out a small squeak and moaned loudly when he pressed it against her clit.

"Don't hold back, babygirl."

Thane was actually surprised by how quickly she came. When he turned off the vibrator, she turned her head, a pink blush coloring her cheeks. "I really needed that."

"Apparently." He leaned down to kiss her. Without breaking the embrace, he turned the wand back on, returning it between her legs. He played with her this time, pulling it back whenever she tensed for an orgasm—building her climax up so it would be more satisfying when she finally released. When he deemed the timing was right, he pressed it against her clit and held it there, thrusting his tongue into her mouth.

Feeling her tense and squirm as her orgasm took over turned him on. He kissed her while she came, burning with desire to claim her.

Afterward, he broke away, giving himself a little space to calm his libido. The last thing Thane wanted was to come before he even had a chance to take her. Chuckling to himself, he told her, "You have my body wound up like a top, babygirl."

"Take me…" she whispered.

He almost lost it, hearing her heartfelt plea. Swallowing down his desire, wanting to play out the scene as he had intended, Thane reached over her to get the rose from off the tray. He plucked off two large petals and placed them on each of her eyelids. It was in homage to a session they'd enjoyed at the Training Center soon after he'd collared her.

"Take in the scent of the blossoms as you concentrate on my touch," he instructed.

Brie smiled when he brushed the rose against her stomach.

"It's so ticklish, Master."

"Take it like a good sub and don't move," he murmured.

Tracing the flower over the soft curve of her neck, he saw the goosebumps it created and smiled to himself. He loved playing with Brie on so many levels.

Feeling devilish, he headed toward her breasts, taking delight when her nipples hardened as he teased them with the soft petals.

Thane traced concentric circles on her stomach and noticed her breathing had become more shallow and rapid.

He teased her body with the rose for several minutes, but found he was too desperate to wait. When he could not hold back his passion any longer, Thane pulled out the tube of lubricant from under his pillow.

Brie lay there, the two rose petals acting as her blindfold, as she waited, unsure what he had planned next.

Putting a generous amount in his hand, he began rubbing his aching cock with it.

When she heard the slippery sound, she moaned loudly.

Thane growled in her ear. "Yes, téa, I am about to fuck that sweet ass of yours."

She arched her back as she rubbed her breasts sensually in anticipation. "Oh, I can't wait to feel you, Master…"

Once his cock was properly lubed, he took the petals from her eyes and told her, "I need you to put up the railing and lay on your side."

He stared at the shapely ass she presented to him as she lay settled beside him. He took a moment to admire its beauty—dragging out the anticipation for them both. He then placed his fingers, still covered in lubricant, against her pink rosette and rubbed against it.

Brie moaned in appreciation.

"You like that?" he murmured lustfully.

"I love it when you touch me there."

"Then maybe you'll like this even more…" He slowly slipped his finger inside and felt her shudder with pleasure.

Had it not been such a long time, he would have played with her, but he seriously needed to sink his cock into that fine ass. Grabbing his rigid shaft, Thane pressed the head of his cock against her tight rosette.

He loved the initial resistance as her body instinctually fought against the invasion. But there always came that moment when it gave into his need and her body relaxed, allowing him to breach the taut opening.

They both voiced their satisfaction as his cock slowly slipped into her. He had not experienced the added tightness six months of pregnancy caused, and found it only served to heighten his experience.

"Oh, babygirl…" Grabbing onto the railing for leverage, he pushed his cock deeper into her.

Brie moaned in pure bliss.

He nuzzled her ear as he began slowly thrusting. Thane knew he wouldn't last much longer, so he picked up the wand. "Hold this against your clit while I fuck this sexy ass."

Brie whimpered in excitement as she turned it on and pressed the toy against her mound. The vibration against his cock was intense, making it nearly impossible to hold back his orgasm.

Thane waited until Brie cried out, her inner muscles milking his cock as she came. It only took a few quick thrusts before he was joining her in his own powerful climax. He pressed his lips against her neck as his body released burst after burst of his seed, leaving him completely and achingly spent after the last thrust.

He wrapped his arms around Brie and lay there, his shaft still inside her, content to soak in the afterglow of their connection.

Thane was surprised to hear Brie crying. "What is it, babygirl?"

She looked back at him, her bottom lip trembling. "I have missed this part of us. It almost hurts, I'm so happy right now."

He leaned over and kissed her tenderly on the cheek. "This is our fresh beginning, téa. I have so much more planned for us in the years ahead."

She gazed into his eyes. "I'm so grateful to call you husband, but I will always think of you as my Master first. I didn't realize that until tonight."

He wiped away the remaining tear from her cheek. "You are all things to me—submissive, lover, friend, wife, and soon-to-be-mother of my child. No matter what name you answer to, be it Brie, téa, babygirl, or little mama, you are the same beautiful soul I fell in love with that night you met me after class."

"I'm so in love with you, Sir."

"I—" He felt his voice catch, overwhelmed by the powerful love he felt for her. "I am hopelessly in love with you."

He leaned forward, their lips meeting halfway.

"Condors," she sighed, contently.

"Until the end of time…"

Brother

Thane felt a tremendous flood of emotion when Durov walked through the door of his hospital room. The man looked terrible, beat up and battered, a skeleton of the burly Russian he knew—but he was *alive*.

The first thing Durov did was to walk up to Brie and put his hand on her stomach. "Oh, *radost moya*, you have grown…"

The heartfelt gesture moved Thane, and it seemed only natural when Durov leaned down to kiss her. But Durov immediately looked over at Thane and apologized. "I am sorry. I couldn't resist."

Thane only smiled, trying to rein in the emotions threatening to overwhelm him. Answering in a gruff voice, he said, "Ah hell, I'd kiss you, too, if that were my thing. Get over here."

Pulling himself into an upright position, Thane embraced his blood brother. He refused to let go, shocked that this day had truly come.

It was literally minutes before the two of them finally let each other go.

Looking at the number of wounds covering his body, Thane exclaimed, "Damn it, man, you look terrible. Seriously terrible."

Brie rushed to embrace Durov, burying her face in his chest. She, too, was in shock and cried, "I can't believe it…"

Durov looked at Thane with a half-grin.

The look of contentment on that broken face seared itself into Thane's mind. No matter his condition, Durov was back, and all was right with the world again.

Thane had experienced this once before with Durov, many years ago, when the Russian had returned to his motherland. Thane had grown worried after losing contact with him days after he'd left the States.

Concerned for Durov's life after the violent confrontation with Samantha, he'd dropped everything and had headed to Russia to find his friend…

"Where is he?" Thane demanded, pounding on Andrev's door.

Durov's brother answered it, looking at Thane in disgust. "No one has seen the bastard, and I don't care if I ever do again. Anton is bad news for this family. Mother is dead, and he spouts crazy talk?"

A deadly chill went through Thane.

After suffering the loss of Tatianna, Thane knew Durov would not be able to handle the death of his beloved mother.

"What happened to her?"

Andrev's mouth curled into a snarl. "She is dead, *psikh*. That is all you need to know."

"Where's Anton?" Thane insisted, not willing to leave until he got the answers he needed.

"I told you—my brother is bad news. We are all better off without him."

Without hesitating or thinking of the consequences, Thane punched the asshole in the jaw and welcomed the pain that shot through his hand as he watched Andrev stagger from the impact.

The man sneered. "Apparently, you are as crazy as Anton." He spat at Thane's feet and turned his back on him.

Thane growled angrily, "He needs our help."

Andrev turned his head, a sarcastic smile on his face. "*Da*, he *is* in need of help. The kind you get in a mental institution for the criminally insane."

Thane wound up for another swing, but Andrev skirted to the side, yelling, "Go back to America, *psikh*. You are not wanted here."

"I'm not here for you."

"If fate is just, Anton is already dead."

Thane saw only red as he rushed Andrev, knocking him to the ground before pummeling his face. If it hadn't been for a couple of beefy neighbors nearby pulling Thane off of him, Andrev would have ended up in the hospital and Thane would have been headed for a Russian prison.

Instead, Andrev brushed himself off as he glared at Thane. "I hope you both get what you deserve." He spat at Thane before walking away.

The encounter with his brother left Thane exactly where he'd started. He still had no idea where Durov was. Panic began to set in, knowing he might be facing another suicide.

Thane looked at the scar on his wrist. Even though Durov had made a solemn vow to him, Thane was afraid that the shock of his mother's murder would prove too much after all he'd been through.

After visiting the popular drinking establishments of Moscow without any success, Thane began walking through the seedier parts of the city, checking the backstreets and alleys along the way.

That's where he finally ran across Durov, sprawled out on the ground, unconscious, his face covered in blood.

Thane asked one of the panhandlers nearby if he knew what had happened to him.

The man shook his head. "You don't want to be around when he wakes up. That one is a berserker. Completely mad."

Thane immediately started slapping Durov's face, "Wake up, Durov! It's Thane. I'm going to get you out of here, but I need you to wake up!"

The panhandler let out a low whistle. "You must have a death wish," he stated as he slowly backed away. "Don't say I didn't warn you…"

Thane shook Durov, relieved to hear a groan escape his lips. That was just before his jaw exploded in pain from a right jab. He grabbed both of Durov's wrists and pinned him to the ground. "It's me, Thane…"

When he saw there was no recognition, he added, "Your brother."

Pain flashed in Durov's eyes as his vision began to clear and he finally recognized who was holding him down. "*Moy droog...*" he croaked.

Durov turned his head away in shame. "Go," he grunted, before he passed out again.

"Like hell I will," Thane growled, pulling Durov up and hoisting him over his shoulder. "I did not come all this way just to be dismissed, you ass."

Several of the panhandlers hissed and spat in Durov's direction as Thane passed them.

"I see you've made friends," Thane joked as he headed to the main street, hoping to hail a cab and hightail it out of there.

It seemed none of the cabbies were willing to pick up an American holding a bloodied Russian over his shoulder.

"Fuck," Thane grumbled when he saw a pair of intimidating men watching him. They were too well kept to belong in this area, which could mean they were part of the *bratva*, an underground organization Durov refused to be involved in.

"What are you doing with this man?" one of them demanded in Russian as they approached Thane.

"I'm taking my friend to my hotel to clean him up."

"You know him?" the man asked in a tone that made it clear he did not believe Thane.

"We're good friends."

"Hah!" The other man snorted. "Tell us his full name, then."

Thane was unsure if it was a trap. But as he watched the two men tensing, ready to take him down, he felt an honest answer was his only option.

"Rytsar Anton Durov."

The man who'd asked raised an eyebrow, but neither of the men stood down.

Thane knew he had either given away Durov's identity to his enemies or these two men were Durov's allies. He was still uncertain which was the case, when one of the men raised his hand, snapped his fingers, and a black car drove up beside them.

The man opened the door and snarled at Thane. "Tell him he'd better keep his promise to Nikolay."

Thane had no idea who Nikolay was or what Durov had promised him, but Thane understood that fortune had smiled on them, so he quickly pushed Durov inside. He rattled off the address of the hotel to the driver, knowing it would be shared with the two men, but he had no choice.

Thane needed to see how bad Durov's injuries were but, first, he had to clean him up.

To Thane's surprise, the driver got out of the car and helped him get Durov into the hotel room. He even lifted Durov into the bathtub while Thane hastily gathered needed supplies.

Before he left, the man informed Thane, "Nikolay has a vested interest in Durov."

"So I keep hearing," Thane mumbled after the man shut the door.

Thane carefully undressed his friend, assessing each wound as he did so. Once he was convinced the wounds were not life threatening, he turned on the water to let the tub fill up.

When the warm water finally covered his chest, Durov opened his eyes.

The pain in those blue eyes was too intense for Thane to bear, and he had to turn away. Echoes of the pain he'd felt when his father died fought their way to the surface. But he forced them back—Durov needed him.

Letting in the deep-seated fear that he was about to witness another suicide would not benefit either of them. Instead, Thane put his focus on facing one obstacle at a time, refusing to let himself think beyond that.

First order of business was to get Durov cleaned up. Thane carefully washed all the dirt, blood, and sweat from his body. Durov silently accepted his ministrations, neither helping nor hindering him. It was as if he'd already given up, lacking the energy to protest.

That terrified Thane. He knew the passionate Russian too well not to be concerned by his silence.

Once he had Durov dried and wrapped in a hotel robe, Thane ushered him to the bed and told him to lie down.

The next order of business was to get some warm food into him.

Then, and only then, would he ask about what had happened.

Thane called room service. Durov wouldn't even look at him as they waited for the food to arrive.

Don't you dare give up on me, Thane thought.

Aloud he said, "We're in this life together, no matter

how bad it gets."

Durov turned his head away.

Once Thane had the bowl of warm soup in his hand, he tried to spoon it into Durov's mouth, but he refused to cooperate and let it dribble down his chin to his chest.

When the familiar aroma of the lemony tanginess of sorrel mixed with the vegetable broth reached the Russian's nose, his nostrils flared slightly.

After a few failed spoonfuls, Durov finally shifted his gaze toward Thane. "What is this? A form of Chinese water torture, but with soup?"

"I need you to eat. So you can either let me continue treating you like a spoiled aristocrat or you can pick up the damn spoon and feed yourself. It's totally up to you but, either way, this soup is going down your throat."

"You always have been a pain in my ass, peasant," Durov growled, taking the spoon from him.

It was a small, but significant, victory.

Thane tired not to stare as Durov slowly consumed the soup. *Schav* had been a favorite dish of Durov's that his mother made when he was a child. Thane hoped it would provide his friend some level of comfort, no matter how slight.

Once the bowl of soup was consumed, Durov set it on the bed stand and threw the spoon across the room.

Thane went to pick it up and walked back to him, holding the spoon out to him. "Did that make you feel better? If so, feel free to chuck it again."

Durov glared at Thane.

Finally, he spoke, but his voice held such agony and despair it gutted Thane.

"I failed her. I shouldn't be here."

"What are you talking about?"

"I went to kill my father. I know he killed *Mamul-ya*...*" Durov hesitated for a moment. It seemed like he was about to say something else, but changed his mind. He looked at Thane, howling in heart-wrenching pain.

Tears of anger filled his eyes as he shared, "The bastard had racked up enough debt to require a sacrifice as payment. And that coward..." his voice grew cold, "he selected my mother to pay."

Thane looked at him in horror and disbelief. "But he loves her."

Fire flashed in Durov's eyes. "He did, which makes his crime more heinous. You sacrifice for those you love—you don't sacrifice them."

"What happened when you confronted your father?" Thane asked, seeing that he was losing Durov to the dark pull of despair.

When he didn't respond, Thane shook him. "What happened?"

Durov spat in disgust, "I was never given the chance to avenge my mother. Nikolay spared his life, and mine."

"I have heard that name mentioned several times today. Who is he?"

"The *Pakhan* of the Koslovs, a powerful clan in Russia."

"Part of the *bratva*?"

"*Da.*"

"I was told you owe him something."

A growl emanated from deep in Durov's chest. "I did not expect to live after my father's death but, because of Nikolay's interference, both he and I are still alive. Life is a cruel joke, *moy droog.*"

"Does he expect you to work for him?" Thane demanded to know. "Is that why you were hiding?"

Durov huffed. "I was not hiding. I was looking for a fight that would end in my death. I no longer want to be here."

"You can't talk like that," Thane warned him.

Durov glanced at Thane, the pain in his eyes now intensified.

"I watched her die, *moy droog*…but was helpless to prevent it. I needed that bastard to die, but I failed in that, too."

"What about your brothers? Why can't they help bring justice for your mother? By God, there are four of them!"

Durov shut his eyes, but could not stop the tears from falling. "That is the greatest cruelty of all. My brothers banned me from her funeral, but let my father attend."

"That makes absolutely no sense."

Durov turned his head slowly, meeting Thane's gaze. "My brothers are cowards like my father. We should all be put out of our misery and rid the world of the Durov taint."

"You are *not* allowed to talk like that."

"I don't want you here. Go home." Durov waved him away dismissively.

Thane pulled up his sleeve and showed Durov the scar. "We are in this together, damn it. Remember, *brother?*"

Durov looked down at the scar, frowning sadly. "I didn't know it would come to this when I made that vow." He put his hand on Thane's shoulder and said solemnly, "I'm sorry, comrade, but I want to die."

Thane felt anger like white fire boiling up inside him. "No, damn it! We vowed that we would be there for each other—and I will not fail you."

Thane got to his feet and demanded Durov stand with him. Putting his hand on the Russian's shoulder, he told him, "You are *not* the coward your father is. You will not only survive this, but you will exact justice for your mother's murder. Someday, the pain of this moment will become the catalyst for you to do great things. I know that both your mother and Tatianna expect you to be strong, to endure, and to live a life that would make them proud."

"You are placing too much on my shoulders, comrade."

"No. I am not, because you're not doing this alone. As your brother, I stand beside you."

He shook his head weakly. "I am tired and broken. I have nothing left."

"Which is why I'm here."

Durov looked deep into his eyes. "Just let me go."

"Never."

"It would be so much easier."

"For you, but not for me."

"You don't understand, *moy droog*. You are doomed if you stay with me."

"I don't care."

Durov's tough exterior crumbled. "I could not handle losing anyone else."

"We will survive this. The minute you give up, you condemn us both."

"That is not fair," Durov complained.

"What? You take a vow and expect me to survive your suicide? That, my friend, is not fair."

"I hate you," Durov growled, upset that Thane wasn't leaving.

"You know, you are a selfish prick."

"Have I ever stated any differently?"

Thane chuckled sadly. "No, but I match your level of selfishness with my stubbornness. I'm like the never-ending waves hitting rocks against the shore. I will wear you down to sand with my unyielding resolve."

Durov snarled. "I already told you the Durov clan is not worth your time."

"Your family is not but *you*, Anton Durov, are."

"Did I express how much I thoroughly dislike you?"

"You mentioned it."

Durov gritted his teeth. "You're not only stubborn, but highly irritating."

"Like a wave against the rock."

"I'm already sick of your wave analogy."

Thane smirked. "Never-ending…"

Durov roared in frustration, hitting the pillow beside him repeatedly with great force.

Thane was heartened to see his anger expressed. He knew as long as he could get a rise out of Durov, they both would be okay.

The two of them had been through so much together, but this latest ordeal had almost destroyed them both.

"Wallace told me you were in seriously bad shape when they found you." Thane looked him over in distress. "But seeing how bad you look now, I can only imagine how serious it really was."

Durov shrugged off his concern. "It could have been worse."

"Yes, you could have died," Thane responded somberly.

"Do not dwell on it, *moy droog*. I am here now."

Thane shook his head, looking at them both. "We're a hell of a mess, you and I."

Durov gave him a crooked grin. "Wait until we are old men, comrade. What stories we will have by then."

Thane shook his head. "No, let's keep it simple. 'They got old, didn't get out much, and lived happily ever after.'"

Durov threw his head back and laughed, clutching his chest in pain.

The Russian's hearty laughter filled the room, lifting Thane's spirits. He looked over at Brie and found her laughing as well.

Yes, truly all was right with the world—once again.

Matter of Trust

Thane was lying in his own bed, grateful to be home and in charge of his recovery. It had been a gift from Durov, who had insisted that Thane get out of the hospital immediately, and then made it happen.

At the time, Thane hadn't appreciated how right Durov was.

Despite the good care he'd received, there was nothing more healing to a man's soul than being in his own home, surrounded by people he loved, eating food he enjoyed, in a familiar and comfortable setting.

In the short time since he'd been back at the apartment Thane was already seeing marked improvements in his mobility—aided by the nurse and therapist who worked with him daily.

Durov had only stayed with them at the apartment for a short time, preferring to move to his beach house and live with his new best friend, Little Sparrow. The pup who'd fed Durov scraps during his imprisonment in Russia, had apparently won over Durov's heart based on what Brie had said.

It hadn't been easy watching him leave. Both Thane and Brie had grown accustomed to his booming voice and passionate ways. However, Durov deserved to forge a life of his own if that was what he truly desired.

Still…the Russian was sorely missed.

So Thane was gratified to hear Durov's familiar voice when he greeted Brie at the door. Soon he heard the sound of his steady stride as it echoed down the hallway toward his room.

"*Moy droog*, we have to get you out of this place," Rytsar insisted as he entered the bedroom.

"I'm doing fine here."

"*Nyet*. You are in sore need of fresh air and sunshine." He looked around the room and shrugged. "This is only slightly better than the hospital."

Brie walked into the room, having overheard their conversation. "I would enjoy soaking up some vitamin D." She looked Thane over and added, "No offense, Sir, but you're starting to have an almost vampirish complexion."

Thane smirked. "Come here, snack. Let me sample that neck of yours."

Brie leaned over and offered her throat to him, giggling when he pressed his teeth against her sensitive neck and bit down.

When he pulled away, he told Durov, "I'm sorry to say that we will have to wait to take you up on that offer. I need to stay focused on my rehabilitation. Until I'm able to get places by my own power, I am not going anywhere."

To illustrate his limited progress, Thane positioned

himself on the edge of the bed before pushing off while using a walker to steady himself. Although he was getting better, he still had a long way to go and did not have the luxury of interrupting his daily routine with a day at the beach.

Thane slowly walked out of the bedroom and headed to his desk. With great effort, he lowered himself into his chair and pushed the walker away, grateful for its stability—but resenting it just the same.

Picking up the letter from a client in Italy, he held it up to Durov. "Rather than spend time relaxing in the sun, I need to get caught up with my clients."

Durov huffed good-naturedly. "You can work anywhere. Come join me, *moy droog.*"

The Russian was persuasive, and Thane considered it for a moment. "No, I can't."

Durov smirked, looking at Brie. "*Radost moya*, convince your man to come."

Thane glanced in Brie's direction and saw that she was staring at the envelope in his hand, a troubled expression on her face. She quickly glanced away when he caught her staring.

"Is there something wrong, Brie?"

She looked down at the floor, avoiding eye contact with him when she answered. "It's nothing, Sir."

He reached out to her. "Tell me what you were thinking just a second ago."

Brie moved over to him, shrugging. "Sir, I had an errant thought and do not wish to talk about it."

"Being open with me is never a mistake," he assured her. He placed his finger under her chin and tilted it up so he could look into her eyes. "Tell me."

Brie shifted uncomfortably as she met his gaze. "I was wondering about the letter Lilly sent you. I remember seeing you tear up an envelope that looked like the one you are holding. You told me it was nothing, but was that untrue, Sir?"

Thane shot a glance at Durov, needing him to leave the room.

The Russian understood and announced loudly, "I will get us vodka. Call when you are ready for me to head back up."

After he left the apartment, Thane nodded toward the couch. He made his way from the desk to the sofa and asked her to sit beside him.

"Before we discuss this any further, understand that the letter I tore up was not from her. It was exactly as I stated—a legal matter involving a client. It did not involve you."

She lowered her eyes, blushing in shame. "I'm sorry, Sir."

"You are right, however, that I should have spoken to you after receiving Lilly's threat to blackmail me. I failed to appreciate the extent of her delusion and how dangerous she truly was."

"We all did."

He caressed her cheek. "I thought it could be handled without incident through Thompson's legal team. There was no point in upsetting you over something so trivial. I never suspected she would be capable of taking it as far as she has. But she did, and that..." His hand dropped to his side as he looked at her with sorrow.

"That is on my shoulders."

"I don't blame you for what happened, Sir. I just didn't expect to be left in the dark when we promised to be open with each other."

Thane wrapped his arms around her, his heart aching. His desire to protect her had almost cost them everything. "I failed to keep my promise to you, Brie."

He was overcome by a sense of remorse and deep shame for breaking her trust. Thane fought the dark thoughts that hovered on the edge of his consciousness, knowing what could have happened. Keeping his voice light, he asked her, "Since rice is not an option due to my current condition, what do you deem a worthy punishment?"

She frowned. "I don't want to punish you, Sir."

"It is something I welcome, and is only fair, téa." By invoking her sub name, he was stressing the importance of honoring his request.

Brie pouted her bottom lip. "But you have been through so much."

"As have you."

She looked at him critically. "If I must, it needs to be something you will never forget, like the rice punishment was for me."

"Agreed."

"But not physically taxing, as I don't want to add more stress to your body or hinder your recovery in any way."

Brie spent a long time thinking about it, but kept shaking her head as if she were dismissing each idea as it came. He would have found it amusing, but for the profound shame he felt.

Finally, Brie gave up in frustration. "I need more time to think about this, Sir."

"That would probably be best, since Durov is still waiting downstairs for a call."

Brie looked at him with alarm. "Poor Rytsar! I completely forgot about him."

"Don't let him know that."

"No," she giggled. "I won't."

"You should be the one to call and let him know it's safe to return. No doubt he's worried and will appreciate hearing from you that everything is okay."

As she got up from the couch, Thane reached out and touched her arm. "It's important to both of us that you choose a consequence for my breach of trust. You need the reassurance I understand my mistake, and I need a physical task to release the guilt I feel."

"I understand, Sir. I've never forgotten how much I hated and appreciated the rice." She smiled mischievously, adding, "However, I don't think like you do. My punishment will be uncomfortable, but in a completely different way."

Brie laughed as she picked up her cell phone to call Durov.

Thane watched her with a critical eye, still concerned.

Brie had endured the wrath of his mother, Ruth, and her attack on Brie's film career. The girl had also suffered through his own dark demons, unleashed after his dealings with Lilly in China. Soon after that, Brie was left fighting to support him both physically and mentally because of the plane crash. At the same time, she was forced to deal with the threat of Lilly.

He'd known the day Brie offered her collar to him that he was unfit as a partner. It was the reason he'd refused initially, even though he desperately loved her.

Unfortunately, everything that had happened since then had only proved he'd been right. And, yet, Brie had remained beside him every step of the way, giving him her heart and devotion without reservation.

She was a remarkable woman—a condor in every sense of the word.

Thane thought back to that moment when he'd doubted her back when she was newly collared and they were still adjusting to their new life as D/s partners.

He'd caught Brie reading his mother's vile note, which he had strictly forbade her from opening. The profound sense of betrayal he'd felt had been all-consuming and had almost destroyed their relation-ship…

"You have betrayed me on a level I'd never thought possible," he told Brie in disbelief.

Striding over to her, Thane snatched the note, crum-pling it into a ball before turning on the gas stove.

"She'll destroy the violin!" Brie blurted.

Thane closed his eyes, hesitating for a second before tossing the paper onto the flame. As it burned, he growled darkly under his breath, turning on her.

"I commanded you not to have any contact with the

beast, and yet I find you here, seeking out her correspondence behind my back. I have purposely disregarded every attempt at contact, and then you do this…?"

He could hear the desperation in her voice, but remained unmoved as she explained, "Sir, I wanted to destroy the note myself."

"The fact that you disobeyed a direct order on something so vital speaks volumes, Miss Bennett."

The girl whimpered and hastily explained, "Sir, your mother threatened Mary and Faelan for not delivering the message. I wanted to protect them—and you—from its contents. But before I destroyed it, I was overcome with hope that she wanted to make things right by you."

Black rage filled his heart. "Things will *never* be right between us!"

Brie fell to the floor, bowing to him. "I'm sorry, Sir."

Her pleas fell on deaf ears, his shock and disgust at her disloyalty making it impossible to deal with her fairly.

Thane asked in an icy tone, "Do you realize what you have done?"

She only shook her head, her forehead remaining pressed to the floor.

"You've forced me to react. Now I am obligated to liberate my father's violin from the beast."

The idea of having to face his mother after everything she had done to him made Thane's insides burn with fury. But, even worse, was having to deal with the emotional betrayal of the woman kneeling before him, the woman he had entrusted his heart to.

Thane knew he had to leave Brie's presence before he did something they would both regret.

Turning his back on her, he headed back to the bedroom to deal with the excruciating pain of the headache he was suffering from, as well as this unwanted complication.

He sat down on the bed, pressing hard against his temples, trying to alleviate the ever-mounting pressure building in his head.

"I should never have collared her," he growled out loud.

But, damn it, I love her…

That day when Thane had told Brie that he was a condor, it wasn't a declaration made in the moment, but a simple statement of fact. Even now, knowing she had disobeyed him on something so fundamentally crucial, he still loved her—he always would.

But how could he ever trust her again?

Thane had wanted to spare them both this emotional nightmare by refusing her collar, but Brie was so genuine in her affection. It was because of her that he had begun to believe love still existed in the world, despite seeing it decimated in his own family.

He sat there, suffering alone in the bedroom in unbearable pain.

Why, Brie? Why would you betray me like this?

Pressing harder against his temples as the pain became intense like white-hot fire, he closed his eyes, contemplating his next step.

He was a condor.

Thane would never love another. If he let Brie go now, he would be condemning himself to a life alone. He had to find a way for them to make it through this together.

He had to—there was no other option.

When Brie hung up the phone after inviting Durov to return, she looked back and caught him reminiscing about that difficult moment in their past.

"What's wrong, Sir?"

He shook his head.

Brie immediately walked over and knelt beside him, placing her hand on his knee. "Please tell me."

He looked at her tenderly. "I was simply remembering where we started, and appreciate how far we have come."

She scolded him gently, "But that would not explain the expression I saw on your face."

Thane cradled her cheek in his hand, gazing into those honey-colored eyes. "I wish being partnered with me didn't have to be so challenging, babygirl. You deserve a carefree and stable life."

She kissed his hand. "I'm grateful to be here with you now—after all we've suffered. It's worth everything it took to get here, because it makes simple moments like these even sweeter. I've never looked back with regret, Sir."

He lifted her hand to his lips. "It is an honor to love you, Mrs. Davis."

Durov returned with two bottles of vodka. "Vodka solves everything," he announced, grabbing two shot glasses and bringing them to the coffee table.

"Sorry, old friend. Neither Brie nor I are drinking alcohol until the baby is born."

His jaw dropped. "What?"

"I felt it was only fair since she is abstaining."

Durov looked at Brie. "Is he serious?"

Brie smiled sympathetically and nodded.

Durov looked at the two bottles forlornly. "But I do not care to drink alone."

Brie got up and headed into the kitchen, coming out with a carton of coconut water and another shot glass. "This is what we drink these days."

"Let me try it."

Brie filled each glass and winked at him as she handed out the shots to each of them.

Durov watched Brie intently as she put the glass to her lips and took a sip. He then turned to Thane. "You really drink this, *moy droog*?"

"*Da,*" Thane answered with a grin, downing the shot and placing the glass on the coffee table. He raised an eyebrow in challenge.

Durov stared at the glass in his hand suspiciously for several moments before tipping it back. He immediately sputtered—a spray of liquid escaping his lips and flying through the air. "That is revolting, comrade!"

Brie giggled as he wiped his mouth with his sleeve, a

nasty expression on his face.

"Don't ever give that to me again," he warned them.

Thane made a mental note to surprise Durov with coconut water at some point in the future.

Brie left the room and came back with a towel. Durov took it from her, cleaning himself first before wiping the floor. "I do not know how I will get that disgusting taste out of my mouth."

Thane opened one of his bottles of vodka and poured a small amount into Durov's glass, swirling it to rinse it out. He poured the used liquid into his own glass before refilling Durov's shot glass with pure vodka. "I'm sure this will help."

Durov gladly took the shot glass and downed it, holding out the empty glass for Thane to refill. "I think two more times will do."

Thane refilled it willingly. The look on Durov's face when he downed the coconut water kept replaying in his mind.

"What are you smiling about, comrade?"

Thane only chuckled, steering the conversation away from the question. "Téa, would you get my belts off the nightstand?"

Brie's eyes widened as she bowed to him before heading down the hallway to their bedroom.

"*Moy droog*, what are you up to?" Durov asked lustfully.

"Although I have no time for a day at the beach, I think a short break will prove refreshing for all three of us."

Brie returned naked, holding the four leather belts

that had lain on his nightstand for months, waiting for use.

Thane took the belts from her, handing three to Durov. "I always say when you can't get drunk on vodka, get drunk on Brie."

Durov took the belts from him and stared at her hungrily. "How should we play with her?"

"Bind her with two of the belts, and you and I will take turns teasing her with the others."

"Oh, I like the way you think, *moy droog*."

"I do, too, Master." Brie grinned as she shifted her gaze to the floor, waiting for their attention.

The first belt he placed over her eyes and measured the needed length before creating a new hole in the leather with the tip of a sharp blade. He placed the belt back over her eyes and cinched it tight. Grabbing the extra length and pulling on it, he forced her head back so he could kiss her on the lips.

"That was my most expensive belt," Thane informed him as they stood, admiring his handiwork.

"You are welcome, comrade."

"Hands to your sides, *radost moya*." Durov commanded as he took the second belt and placed it just under her breasts, binding her arms against her body. He leaned forward and tweaked one nipple, telling Thane, "This way we can thoroughly enjoy those impressive breasts."

Thane made his way over to Brie, and asked, "How do you like being blind and bound, knowing two men are about to play with you?"

"I like it very much, Master."

"Even though we will be using belts?"

He remembered her initial aversion to them, believing belts were a form of punishment—not pleasure.

She hesitated. "I trust you with belts, Master."

"And Durov?"

A small sigh escaped her lips.

Thane glanced over at his friend, who was grinning.

Durov leaned toward her and said in a low, sultry voice, "*Radost moya*, I will show you how a man loves a woman with his belt."

Brie moaned softly.

"Guide her to the window," Thane instructed Durov. "I want her to feel the cold chill of the glass as she presents herself to the world."

Durov took her arm and guided her to the expansive window overlooking LA. Thane came up behind, and pressed his hand against her upper back, gently forcing her to lean forward so her breasts made contact with the cool glass. She let out a small gasp.

"Press your cheek against the window for balance, but do not let any other part of your body, including that sweet, round belly of yours, touch the glass," he told her.

Brie adjusted herself, leaning forward, her ass now properly presenting itself—begging to be whipped.

Thane stood back, appreciating the look of his submissive. Her arms were bound to her sides with his dark brown belt, her eyes covered in black leather with the tail end trailing down her back invitingly, and those succulent breasts pressed against the window.

Brie's bare skin beckoned to him and he nodded to Durov. "Make love to her with the belt."

Thane headed back to the couch, needing to rest before his turn. He had no problem sitting back to observe their exchange.

Durov folded the belt in his hand into a loop. Rather than striking her with it, he let it glide over her skin as he whispered to her. Thane could see Brie physically relaxing as his friend used the belt like an extension of his body, caressing her skin with it.

"*Radost moya*, give into my love for you…"

He glided the belt over her legs and thighs, back and shoulders, taking special care to lightly caress her neck and lips with the leather. By the time he was finished, she had goosebumps on her skin.

Durov looked back at him, letting him know his turn had come. "Now let your man love you," he growled.

Before he left Brie, Durov gave her a single snap of the belt on her ass.

She cried out from the unexpected lash and then giggled nervously.

Thane returned to her, letting his hands begin their dance over her skin before he applied the belt. "You are a beautiful girl," he whispered huskily. Moving to the other ear he said, "You are a good girl…"

Brie purred, "Thank you, Master."

Thane stood beside her, pulling on the blindfold to force her head back. It caused Brie to arch her back as her chest became the sole contact with the glass.

She was now dependent on him to keep her balanced, as he held the blindfold tight and gave her the first lash of his belt. He watched her skin dance from the contact as the satisfying crack of the belt filled the room.

"Color, téa?"

"Green, Master."

"Harder?"

"Yes, please."

He alternated his strokes, pinkening both buttocks. When his muscles began complaining, however, he lowered his belt, pulling harder on the blindfold to tilt her head and give her a passionate kiss.

He gently released the hold he had on the blindfold so she could settle back against the glass, and then ran his hand over her ass, growling in admiration.

Durov seemed inspired after watching their exchange, and took the belt from Thane, grinning at him as he told Brie, "I have loved you with the belt, and now I will astound you."

"Oh…" she said, a hint of fear in her voice.

"Tell me what you want, *radost moya*," he demanded.

"I want you, Rytsar."

"You mean my belt?" he teased.

"And your belt."

Durov stepped away from her, a folded belt in each hand. He positioned himself behind Brie and stared hungrily at her ass.

He glanced back at Thane and winked.

Thane shook his head, knowing it was not a good idea, but Durov was a stubborn soul.

Using the belts like dual floggers, he began striking Brie double time with the leather. Just as she started squeaking in pleasure, he froze up.

Durov was forced to stop because of the pain and looked over at Thane for help.

Thane gestured to the tantra chair, and Durov nodded his agreement.

He laid his large hand on Brie's ass and said in a deep, guttural tone, "You are a good girl, *radost moya*. Do you know what happens to good girls where I come from?"

She shook her head.

"They get punished."

Brie whimpered.

"Come."

Brie obediently followed him, although her fear was easy to read.

Durov left her standing by the tantra chair as he slowly undressed. Thane followed his lead, and soon, both men were naked, standing together, staring at Brie.

Without speaking, Thane laid down on the tantra chair while Durov help guide her wet pussy onto his hard cock.

Durov then sat behind Brie on the tantra chair, fingering her ass while Thane enjoyed her spirited up and down motion as she thoroughly fucked his cock.

Pulling on the belt around her eyes, Durov brought her lips to him and kissed her as he eased his thumb into her ass.

"When you are no longer with child, I will be pounding this ass while you fuck your Master."

Brie moaned, seeking his mouth again, needing his kiss.

"Until then, I will content myself with this." Durov released the belt and wrapped his arm around her to play with her clit.

Thane watched Brie tense. The combination of his

cock deep in her pussy, Durov's thumb in her ass, and his fingers vigorously rubbing her clit, proved too much and she cried out, "Master, I'm about to come!"

Thane nodded to Durov.

The Russian bit down on her throat, and her whole body seemed to freeze. Growing still, both men waited. A few seconds later her body exploded in a forceful orgasm.

Thane held her tight, savoring the strong muscle contractions as her body coaxed his own orgasm. He began to pump her, wanting Brie to feel his orgasm during the last pulses of hers.

After he was spent, Durov lifted Brie off and pushed her against the higher end of the tantra chair. He coated his cock with lubricant.

With his other hand wrapped around her throat, he asked Brie. "Do you remember the first time I claimed you?"

"Yes, my warrior."

He growled lustfully, spreading her ass cheeks apart before slowly penetrating her tight hole. Thane changed positions, grasping the back of her head while Durov still held her throat.

Kissing her deeply, Thane ravaged that mouth with his tongue, then teased and tugged on her nipples as Durov fucked her in the ass.

The two men worked in unison, dominating her body for hours.

Vile Flower

Thane didn't want to end Lilly's life, which Durov strongly advised he do. However, he agreed with his friend that she would remain a threat to Brie until her dying breath.

Before he could make a decision, Thane needed to assess Lilly's mental state himself. Although he was not strong enough to stand for long periods of time, he decided to go to the Tatianna's Legacy Center, known as the TLC, where Lilly was being contained. It was the facility for survivors of human trafficking Durov had funded, run by Stephanie Conner, the girl he had saved in Russia.

Thane had asked Wallace to drive him, but planned to sit there alone and secretly listen in on Lilly for several hours. It was critical that he evaluate the situation himself, without the influence of others.

What he hadn't anticipated was how difficult it would be for Brie—this visit with Lilly. When the doorbell rang, Brie looked at him nervously as she went to answer it.

"It's good to see you again, Wallace," Thane called out, pushing his wheelchair forward to greet him.

"Likewise, Sir Davis," he said, shaking Thane's hand. He glanced at Brie and asked, "Hey, you don't mind if I steal him away from you for a few hours, do ya?"

"No, of course not," Brie replied, but Thane didn't miss the way she fiddled with her hands, her body giving away her true feelings.

The two of them had already discussed this at length beforehand, and Brie understood and agreed with the necessity of Thane doing this. However, she was left having to fight against her justifiable fear of Lilly and her concern for Thane's safety.

"I won't be gone long," he assured her. "And you know there will be no contact with Lilly. I'm just there to assess."

She laughed self-consciously. "I know I shouldn't worry."

"Brie, it might make it easier if you call one of your friends to keep you company until we return," Wallace suggested.

Brie shook her head, smiling. "I can handle this. Really."

Thane gestured to her to kneel beside him.

He caressed Brie's cheek tenderly, feeling her pain. "It's normal for you to be worried after all that has happened. I have similar concerns about leaving you, babygirl. But you and I must work through our fears, so they don't end up controlling our lives."

"I understand in my head what you are saying, but I don't know how to convince my heart, Sir."

He smiled, leaning forward to kiss her. "I don't either, but we'll figure it out as we go."

When Brie stood back up, Thane advised her, "Call a friend. It will help pass the time."

Brie pursed her lips and looked at him thoughtfully. "I should probably call Mary. She's got some explaining to do about the way she's been acting." Brie gave Wallace a sympathetic glance. "And I'm certain she will keep me distracted."

Thane knew that Mary was spending the evening at the TLC dealing with Lilly. However, he could tell no one, not even Brie, about Mary's involvement. That information had to remain a closely guarded secret for Mary's own protection.

"If not her," he said casually, "then I'm sure there are others who would be happy to help you pass the time."

Brie nodded, adding a smile to ease his concern for her. "Well, if Mary won't talk to me, there's always Lea or…even the infamous Ms. Clark."

He chuckled. "I'm sure either would prove entertaining for completely different reasons."

Brie turned her attention back to Wallace. "Please take good care of him," she pleaded.

"You know I will, blossom."

Thane appreciated Wallace keeping things light. There had been a time when he'd had his suspicions about the man, but now he had complete confidence in Wallace—until he tried to touch Thane's wheelchair.

"No!" Thane lashed out. He pushed himself toward the door, but slowed to a stop and turned, needing to explain himself. "Look, I'm not going to recover unless I do things for myself."

"Got it," Wallace said. "No harm, no foul. Last thing I want is people accusing me of making Sir Thane Davis soft."

When the doors to the elevator opened, Thane wheeled himself inside, turning around awkwardly. "I can't wait to get out of this damn chair."

"Why not get a motorized one?"

"I'm determined to build muscle."

"Ah, that makes sense."

As the elevator doors closed, Thane changed the subject, "I never fully thanked you for what you did for Brie in my absence."

"No need. I owed you both."

"I don't think you appreciate what it meant to me."

"You're wrong there," Wallace stated. "I would feel the same if our roles were reversed and it was Kylie."

"Point well taken. Nevertheless, it's important you know how grateful I am. Having Brie safe both physically and emotionally during an extremely stressful time when I was unable to take care of her is…priceless to me."

Wallace pressed the stop button on the elevator and turned to him. "Do you ever get the feeling that things play out exactly how they are meant to? That events happen in our lives in order to prepare us for what's to come? Take Brie as an example. I loved her, I really did, and I changed the course of my sorry life so I could claim her. As you are well aware, I was devastated when she chose you. However, that closeness she and I shared

165

allowed me to care for her after Durov was taken. I would have been clueless as to how to help Brie if I hadn't known her so well. The fact is, Kylie was my destiny, but I wouldn't have met her if Brie hadn't made that documentary. Looking back on it, it all seems to fit together, even though I couldn't see that at the time."

Thane understood what he was saying, but shared his own take on things. "While I appreciate your perspective, I come from the standpoint that we suffer and learn through our circumstances in life. But, in the end, it's *our* choice whether we use those experiences for good or not."

"You don't believe in a higher power?"

"I've vacillated and still remain unsure. But I will say this, I should have died and was given a second chance. It's hard not to feel gratitude toward God, Fate, or whatever it was that was responsible for bringing me back."

Wallace nodded, pressing the button to continue their descent.

"What are your thoughts concerning Lilly?"

Wallace answered him with a frown. "She is a hard case. Mary has told me that she, herself, has been deeply affected by learning about the tragic experiences the girls at the center have suffered. However, when she's shared them with Lilly, the woman appears unmoved."

"I was afraid of that."

"You're right to reserve your judgement until after you've observed her yourself. You know Lilly better than any of us."

Thane growled under his breath. "If she is anything

like my mother, there may be no hope. However, the consequence, if that proves true, disturbs me on a level I can't express."

"I don't envy your position."

When the doors opened, Wallace insisted Thane go out first.

"I don't need special treatment," Thane grumbled as he pushed his wheelchair out.

Wallace snorted. "I wasn't giving any to you. I respect you, Sir Davis, and would have done the same regardless whether you were in a wheelchair or not."

Thane sighed irritably, frustrated with himself. "I suppose I need to stop thinking others see me as helpless."

"'Helpless' is not a word I would ever use to describe you. We all admire your strength and determination."

"Funny...I would have said the same about you."

Wallace clapped him on the shoulder. "As far as I am concerned, you will always be my superior. You did train me, after all."

"Frankly, I had no idea then just how far you would come."

"I owe my growth to you and Brie, as well as Marquis Gray and Nosaka. I've made it a point to never forget where I came from. It helps me keep the right perspective."

"Yet again, I find myself impressed, Wallace."

Wallace shook his head, grinning as he opened the car door for Thane and waited while Thane attempted to maneuver himself into the car. He struggled to lift himself from the wheelchair into the seat, but found his muscles were still too feeble. It was humiliating, but he finally asked for assistance and suffered the indignity in silence.

Once they reached the TLC, Thane was forced to bear a second humiliation as he struggled to get out of the old Mustang. "This is ridiculous," he growled in frustration, having to request Wallace's help again.

"Give it time," Wallace said, lifting him into the wheelchair.

Thane only growled in response.

Once inside, he pushed his wheelchair toward the elevators, stating, "I'll take it from here, Wallace."

"You sure you don't want me to walk you to the room?"

"I know the number, so I see no need," he replied irritably. Thane suddenly realized how he must sound, and explained, "Listen, I don't want Lilly to hear anyone outside her door. I fear it might influence her conversation with Mary."

"Suits me. Meet you back here in two hours?"

Thane nodded.

As Wallace walked out the door, Thane called to him. "Wallace, I don't mean to take my anger out on you."

"Don't give it a second thought. Frustration is part of the healing process. Believe me, I know."

Thane watched as Wallace left the building and made his way to his old Mustang. When the car drove off, Thane turned his wheelchair around and pressed the elevator button.

For all his bravado with Wallace, the truth was Thane

felt nervous about this encounter with Lilly, and what he would discover.

Following the numbers in a maze of hallways, he finally reached the back of the building where Lilly was being held. He wheeled his chair along slowly, careful not to make a sound. He could hear the girls were already talking as he pulled up to the door.

Mary's voice floated down the quiet hallway, speaking with a slight Middle Eastern accent to keep the ruse that they being held somewhere overseas.

"Go ahead, hit me with another one," Lilly insisted.

"Well... there's this girl, Jael. She said they tied her up, legs spread apart. The man who owned her thrust a brush with steel bristles into her repeatedly so she would never have children." Mary's voiced caught for a moment when she shared, "The girl was only twelve, Lilly. She told me that she bled for weeks afterwards. Almost died because of what he did."

"Well, I totally blame the parents," Lilly said dismissively. "If they were too weak to protect their own child, their bloodline needs to end with her. Probably for the best."

"You're a callus bitch, aren't you?"

"Look, I don't understand why you care so much."

"It's pure evil to abuse children. Pure. Unadulterated. *Evil.*"

"And you think any of it matters?" Lilly laughed sarcastically. "Don't you get it? We live in a dog eat dog world. I really don't give a shit what happens to other people. There's only one person I care about—maybe two."

Mary growled with disgust. "The first being you, of course."

"Goes without saying."

"Then let me ask you, because I'm really curious."

"Go on," Lilly encouraged her, sounding as if she was enjoying the direction their discussion was taking.

"If you have so little sympathy for people, why would you ever expect anyone to give a crap about you?"

"Got a rise out of you, did I? Too fucking easy…"

Mary grumbled angrily and fell silent.

Since Mary knew that Thane was there to listen in on the conversation to assess Lilly's mental and emotional state, he had to trust she would get Lilly to open up if he remained patient.

"And I thought I had a cold heart…" Mary complained with a sarcastic tone, finally breaking the silence.

"It has nothing to do with the heart, sweet cheeks, and *everything* to do with the mind. The strong get what they want, and the weak get what they deserve."

"You really believe that?"

"I don't just believe it, I live it."

It was Mary's turn to laugh. "Okay. Then, how do you explain being locked up in here?"

"A bump in the road. I'll figure things out and when I do—people will pay."

Thane felt a chill course through his veins. It was painfully obvious Lilly had no sympathy for others, and had zero remorse for her own actions.

Lilly's tone suddenly became serious when she asked Mary, "Do you know what makes it so easy for me to manipulate others?"

"No."

"People like you."

Mary growled irritably. "Don't be a bitch. I thought we were friends."

"'Friends' is a stretch. But it's true—I like you. And I would like you even *more* if you helped me get out of this fucking place. I have business to take care of."

"What? Finding that Russian dude?"

"Yes, he definitely needs to go first. I won't be able to think straight until he's out of the picture, and I plan to make that fucker pay big time for what he did. I'm thinking a little filleting of the skin would be a nice start, done to a backwards rendition of "You Are My Sunshine"—that bizarre song he was obsessed with. For all his masculine swagger, that song proves he's just a big man-child." She chuckled harshly. "Hell, he proved what a coward he was when he failed to finish the job. Now I get to turn the tables, and I always finish what I start."

"But you're alive because he spared you."

"Which only proves I'm stronger than he is. He deserves to die.

"So if the Russian's first, then the girl must be next."

Lilly answered with venom in her voice. "Was there ever any question? Fuck…I dream about torturing her."

"I know you do."

"But my newest idea may be my best yet."

"Okay, what now?"

"I'm thinking of playing a game of cat and mouse. I'm going to make her think that I'm sorry for what I've done to her. I'll play the repentant wimp for as long as it takes to get that self-righteous cunt to trust a lowly worm like me. I'll beg her to tell me what I can do to make it up to her."

"And this serves what purpose?"

"It'll be entertaining, for one thing, and will get me in the good graces of my lover."

Thane felt an icy chill, knowing she was talking about him.

"Just when she feels safe, I'll turn the knife on her. I will twist and pervert everything she wanted me to do, so that, by the end, she will beg to die. And the best part?"

Mary hesitated for a moment. "What?"

"I won't lay a hand on her."

Mary blew her a loud, audible raspberry. "That's got to be the *lamest* idea you've had yet."

"You don't get it, do you?"

Thane closed his eyes, the blood throbbing in his head, certain he already knew what she was going to say…

Lilly's tone became ominous when she said, "Everything I want to do to her, I'm going to do to the baby while she watches."

Mary's growl was low and menacing.

"What?" Lilly laughed. "You got a problem with that?"

"You *know* how I feel about hurting children."

"Yeah, I know it is a sensitive subject for you." Lilly added with a cruel laugh, "…Daddy's girl."

"Fuck off and die!" Mary yelled.

After several minutes of silence, Lilly couldn't take it anymore and called out. "I was only teasing. Still friends, right?"

Mary said nothing.

Time passed. Eventually, Lilly broke the silence again. "You know, neither of us are getting out of here alone."

Thane knew it was the *only* reason Lilly was interested in continuing a relationship with the girl on the other side of the wall. Relationships meant nothing in Lilly's world. People were commodities, their value marked only by what they could provide for her.

He knew this because he could have very easily fallen into that same mindset. It was disturbing how similar they were. While he understood her line of thinking, every aspect of it sickened him.

Thane looked at his watch and realized Wallace must be upstairs waiting for him. Not needing to hear more, he silently wheeled himself back to the elevator. When he arrived upstairs, he found Wallace standing in the lobby.

Thane growled angrily. "We will need to set up a time for all of us to talk."

"What the hell happened tonight?"

"Based on what I heard, Lilly is beyond saving."

Wallace looked concerned. "What are you planning to do then?"

"I'm not sure, but we are doing no good keeping her here."

"I am sorry to hear that."

Thane looked at him with compassion, knowing this had been Wallace's idea. He assured him by saying, "Trying to rehabilitate her was the right approach. I do not regret that we tried. It eliminates any doubt about what needs to happen now."

"Sir Davis."

Thane met Wallace's gaze, noting the gravity of his tone.

"What one man can live with is not the same as another man."

"Please elaborate."

"Durov is someone who could put Lilly down and not give it a second thought. I am not and, I suspect, neither are you."

"Yes, therein lies the quandary. Even if I had Durov end her life, the blood would be on my hands—the decision mine."

"Exactly. You must decide what you can live with."

"I am not a killer, but I wouldn't hesitate to pull the trigger on Lilly to protect Brie and the baby."

"I understand that."

Thane reached into his pocket and pulled out his phone. "Babygirl, it looks like I'm going to be a little late, and I didn't want you to worry." He heard the concern in her voice when she replied, and told her, "We're heading back now. You and I have a lot to talk about."

After he hung up, Wallace asked, "I don't mean to step out of line, but this might be more than Brie can handle with her due date coming up."

Thane sighed heavily. "I made her a promise. She deserves to know the truth."

"Well, she's certainly tough enough, but it's a damn shame she has to bear this burden."

"I couldn't agree more," Thane stated, pushing himself angrily toward the door.

When he found himself struggling to get into that goddamn fucking car he wanted to rage on something. However, Thane forced himself to breathe, holding back his frustration and mounting anger.

This was a waste of energy.

Self-pity was a luxury he could ill afford. Thane needed to concentrate on every movement he *could* make and build on it—every day. The rest would have to fall to the wayside.

Brie needed a man who could protect her *and* their little baby from any threat.

He was determined, come hell or high water, to be that man.

Keeping His Promise

Thane and Wallace returned to the apartment to find Brie pacing.

When Thane wheeled himself into the apartment, she ran over to him, checking him over as if she expected to see wounds on his body.

"What's all this about?"

"I don't know. I just got a really bad feeling before you called, and I couldn't shake it until I saw you in person."

Thane looked at Wallace with concern.

He pulled her into his lap and held her close. "We're going to be okay, Brie."

She lifted her head from his shoulder to look at him. "Something's seriously wrong."

"Yes," he answered truthfully. "Normally, in this kind of situation, I would spare you the details until I had a better handle on it. However, I am honoring my promise to you."

"Did Lilly escape?" she asked in horror.

"No, babygirl. You're safe, but the situation is grim."

She glanced at Wallace. "It's bad, isn't it?"

He just nodded, looking at her with sympathy.

Brie swallowed hard and turned back to Thane, a whimper escaping her lips.

"I do not believe rehabilitation is possible."

Her face lost all color. "You're not planning to...?" Her voice trailed off, a horrified expression on her face.

Thane was blunt. "I'm weighing every option, given the severity of the situation."

"But, Sir..."

He nodded to Wallace. "I want to thank you for your help tonight."

"Anytime. I'll get out of your hair, but let me know when the others can meet and I'll be there."

"Of course," Thane answered.

Before Wallace left, he told Brie, "I'm sorry my plan didn't work. I was hoping for a better outcome for everyone."

She looked up at him, her bottom lip trembling. "So was I."

Wallace nodded, clearly unhappy. He headed out the door without looking back.

Thane cupped Brie's chin and gazed into her eyes. "I will keep you safe, no matter what it takes."

"I'm scared for us, Sir," she whispered.

"We'll be okay."

"Just knowing Lilly is out there terrifies me but, if she dies, *we* will be responsible." Brie looked down at her belly. "Our baby can't live under the shadow of such violence."

Thane's blood began to boil, thinking about what

Lilly planned for their baby. Whether she would follow through with it remained to be seen, but the fact that she was contemplating it…

"Brie, she has absolutely no remorse for what she's done, and she plans to do worse if she escapes."

"What did you hear?"

Thane looked at her with concern, worried for her well-being. This seemed like one of those times when keeping the truth to yourself could be considered a mercy, but he forged on.

"As you know, I did not speak with her, I simply listened in on the conversation she was having with the informant. But, Brie, what she said has me so upset and angry I cannot voice it aloud—not yet. I'm sorry." He closed his eyes, trying to rein in the black, seething hatred he held for Lilly. The need for action hard to ignore.

Brie placed her hand on his jaw and looked into his eyes with a mixture of fear and compassion.

Thane cleared his throat. "Suffice to say, she is adamant about hurting Durov, you, and the baby."

"Now she's after Rytsar, too?"

"The *one* good thing I heard the entire evening was that Lilly is terrified of Durov." He wrapped his arms around her. "Rytsar can handle himself, but I worry for our informant. Lilly is demented and dangerous. I don't know what to do."

Brie shuddered in his arms. "But we can't become what she is, Sir."

"It would be out of self-defense."

"How would we be any different, then? It doesn't

feel right, Sir. Not when it's done in cold blood."

He understood her reasoning, because he was struggling with that same issue. "I think you should attend the meeting, but I will need to speak to the informant first. She was promised anonymity but, due to the seriousness of this situation and the fact it revolves around you, I feel it is necessary that you be there."

"I agree, Sir. We have to remain united. If we aren't, this will tear us apart."

"I know, babygirl," he murmured, pressing her head against his chest.

Thane closed his eyes, still reeling from Lilly's depravity, and made a silent vow.

I will do anything to protect you—anything.

Thane was grateful to Mary, who encouraged him to bring Brie to the meeting. They gathered at the Training Center in a hidden secret room only a select few knew about.

Since all five were part of the Center, being there would raise no suspicions, and the only person who understood the reason behind the gathering was Marquis Gray.

"Mr. and Mrs. Davis, what a pleasant surprise to see you," Rachel said when she saw them approaching the front desk.

She smiled at Sir, welcoming him with the standard greeting she'd given him for five years, "Good afternoon, Sir Davis."

"And the same to you, Rachel."

"I'm so glad to see you again," she gushed, having not seen Thane since the plane crash.

"Hopefully, the next time I come, I will be walking without any assistance." He took Brie's hand and kissed it. "But I consider myself a fortunate man to have such a beautiful woman to wheel me about."

Rachel gazed at him affectionately. "Oh, Sir Davis, the Center hasn't been the same without you."

Thane didn't miss the look of guilt in Brie's eyes after hearing Rachel's comment. He knew that Brie felt responsible for him stepping down as Headmaster. Squeezing her hand reassuringly, he glanced at Brie's stomach and told Rachel. "As you can see, Brie and I have been keeping ourselves busy."

"Congratulations to you both. I couldn't be happier for you."

"Thank you. Rachel, do you know if Mr. Wallace has already arrived?"

"He has, Sir Davis."

"Excellent. I'm sure Headmaster Anderson is keeping you on your toes."

"And in stitches," she added with a smile. "Have a good day, you two. I can't wait to meet Baby Davis in the near future."

Brie wheeled Thane into the open elevator, telling him how wonderful it was to see Rachel again but, once the doors were closed, she immediately grew quiet and started fidgeting.

"Do you trust me, Brie?"

She stopped and put her hands behind her back. "Of course, Sir."

"Then there is no reason to be anxious. You believe knowledge is power, correct?"

"Yes, Sir."

"Then we will take what we learn today and make the best decision possible for everyone."

Brie leaned against the wheelchair and kissed him soundly on the lips just as the doors opened.

"There is no fraternizing with the students."

Thane looked up and smirked at Gray.

Gray held his hand out to him. "It is good to see you in these halls again, Sir Davis."

"Thank you, Gray. I trust the newest session is going well?"

"The class is providing a challenge, but when do they not?" Gray glanced at Brie, smiling warmly.

When she did not respond, he asked, "Is everything okay, Mrs. Davis?"

She laughed nervously. "I'm sorry, I'm a little distracted."

"Is there something I can help with? Another flogging session, perhaps?"

"That is an excellent suggestion," Thane replied.

Gray looked Thane over with a critical eye. "You could use one yourself."

Gray stared at Thane as if expecting an answer. When none came, he said, "I would give it careful consideration, Sir Davis. You'd be surprised how enlightening it can be."

Thane nodded, mulling the idea over in his head.

"Thank you for the offer, Gray."

"Of course, Sir Davis. Now, you both must excuse me. I have a small matter to attend to." Gray hit the button on the elevator and turned, staring at Thane intently as the doors shut.

"That man is far too clairvoyant," he muttered.

"I've always felt that way," Brie agreed. "I can't hide anything from Marquis."

The hallways echoed with life and excitement, bringing back a flood of memories for Thane. "Do you miss it, Brie?"

Her voice was wistful when she answered. "I do, Sir. I had so many good times here." She then braved asking him, "Do you miss it?"

"When I think of my life then, and what I have now, I realize how empty it was. So, no, I do not miss it."

She looked at him with an expression of gratitude.

"Only speaking the truth, babygirl."

Their last turn led them to a lone door at the end of the hall. Thane knocked on the door twice and waited. Wallace came to the door and quietly ushered them inside, locking the door behind them.

"It's about time, comrade," Durov complained. "We have been waiting for you."

"It is not our fault we were detained several points along the way."

"Well, I blame the cheese," said a familiar female voice.

"Mary?" Brie cried out in surprise.

The Russian stepped aside to reveal Mary standing behind him.

She walked up to Brie with a half-smile. "Yep, stinky cheese. It's your old nemesis."

Brie stared at her in shock. "You're the informant?"

Mary nodded, her eyes naturally gravitating to Brie's round belly.

Brie didn't hesitate and crushed Mary against her. "I didn't know…"

Mary seemed uncomfortable by Brie's public display and stood there awkwardly. "Of course, you didn't know. Nobody knows."

But Mary suddenly seemed to have a change of heart and wrapped her arms around Brie. "Seriously, I can't tell you how good it is to see you looking so round and healthy."

Brie laughed. "And all this time, I just thought you were just being a bitch."

"You're not wrong. I'm still a bitch."

"But you…" Tears filled Brie's eyes. "You did this to help me."

Mary stood back, and bumped her shoulder. "Oh, don't go making a big deal out of it."

Wallace told Brie, "When Mary knew you needed help, she insisted on being a part of it."

Brie turned back to her. "How can I ever—?"

"Family looks out for family, and you happen to be the only family I've got. All I need from you is to have that baby and enjoy your motherhood. That's it, nothing more. End of story."

"But I don't know what to say…"

"Tell me to fuck off. I really *have* been a shitty friend."

"But you risked your life…"

Mary pointed her finger at Brie. "Don't!"

Brie looked at Thane helplessly.

"Go with a simple thank you," he suggested.

"Thank you, Mary Quite Contrary."

Mary burst out laughing. "Well, now, that's more like it."

"Now that *radost moya* has been introduced to the informant, let's get down to business," Durov insisted.

They sat at a round table, allowing them to face each another. Durov sat on the other side of Brie, seeming anxious for Thane to speak. Thane looked at each of them, grateful to have their opinions.

"Before I begin, did Mary tell you all what happened last night?"

"No, Sir Davis. I felt it best that you inform them," she answered.

"Very well." He took a deep breath before beginning. "As you are aware, I went to listen in on Mary's conversation with Lilly. I intended only to assess her, hoping to glean information on how to proceed from here."

Everyone nodded.

"I had hoped Lilly would benefit from the arrangement, but that does not seem to be the case." Thane glanced at Brie. "As Mary can attest, Lilly's hatred for Brie has reached a new and disturbing level. But it is not just Brie that she's after now."

Thane turned to Durov. "If she escapes, she voiced her plans to kill you first."

Durov burst out laughing. "*Da*…I would like to see

her try."

"Although I agree that you are able to defend your-self, I still have concerns. We have no idea who she might enlist to help her if she were to escape at some point. An attack could come from anywhere."

"Do not worry about me, *moy droog*," Durov assured him. "I have survived many fights."

"What did she say about Brie?" Wallace asked. "You seemed quite upset last night."

Thane took Brie's hand, knowing what he was about to share would devastate her and enrage everyone in the room.

"Keep in mind, she was sharing this with Mary, and we cannot know if she would actually carry it out…" The blood in his veins started pounding, and he had to force out the words. "She expressed the desire to kidnap both Brie and the baby for the purpose of torturing the child in front of Brie."

Durov stood up so abruptly, his chair fell backward. "The creature will *not* lay a finger on the babe!"

The anger in Durov's eyes reflected exactly how Thane felt. In a voice filled with rage, he confessed to them, "All I wanted to do is break down the door and choke her to death."

Thane suddenly felt Brie's arms wrap around him. He held her close, trying to rein in the fury burning in his heart.

"I nearly broke my cover when she said that," Mary said. She looked Brie in the eye. "That bitch isn't going anywhere near your baby. I'll fucking choke her myself."

Thane sighed heavily. "I need to decide what to do

with my half-sister before she hurts anyone else."

Durov didn't hesitate. "A rabid dog must be put down."

"No, Rytsar," Brie cried. "We can't…"

He faced her, shaking his head in disagreement. "I fought too hard to get back to have anything happen to you." He laid his hand on her stomach protectively, and added, "Or *moye solntse*."

Thane addressed Wallace next. "Your thoughts?"

"I honestly believe while *murdering* her—and that's what we are talking about here—may eliminate the threat, the cost of it emotionally may prove too much for some involved."

"Brie?" Thane asked, wanting everyone to hear her thoughts because, for him, her opinion was the most important.

Gripping her stomach, she told the group, "I will protect this baby with my life. You know how scared I am of Lilly, but…I can't bear the thought of her being murdered. It would haunt me forever."

Thane put his arm around her, loathing the fact that it was because of his tainted lineage that she was in this situation.

"Mary, what is your opinion?"

"I'm with Rytsar one hundred percent. As long as she lives, she will be a threat to Brie and anyone associated with her. However, hearing what Fae—" She immediately amended her address. "I mean, after hearing what Mr. Wallace and Brie had to say, I wonder if eliminating her will cause a different set of issues."

"No one needs to know what I do," Durov stated

firmly.

Brie laid her hand on his chest. "But I will know, and it will break me inside."

"Do not say that," he pleaded gruffly.

Thane knew Durov was thinking of Tatianna, and was probably now worried he would lose Brie, too, if he were to intervene with Lilly.

This seemed an impossible situation. Thane's gut reaction was to kill her, but he wasn't a murderer. Brie was right on that count.

"What about you?" Wallace asked him.

"I want the threat eliminated. I will not be able to rest until I know beyond a doubt that Brie and the baby are permanently safe from Lilly."

"So, the way I see it, we have two yeses, two nos, and a maybe," Mary said.

"There must be a way," Thane insisted, wanting to calm the desperation he saw in Brie's eyes.

The room was silent for several minutes before Durov spoke up. "We need to make her disappear."

Wallace's eyes flashed with excitement. "And we can!"

"How?" Thane asked.

"An American without money or a passport can become a prisoner in certain parts of the world."

"Yes!" Mary agreed. "It's happened to countless girls at the TLC."

"Hmm…" Durov said, pondering the suggestion, "I do know of a few people who would be glad to take her."

"No, no, no!" Brie cried. "We won't subject her to

the same horrors Tatianna suffered."

"I would not!" Durov objected. "I may want the creature dead, but I am no monster."

"What, then?" Thane asked, now encouraged by this new line of thinking.

"In my country, there are establishments that only seek slave labor."

"But I don't want her to be abused," Brie insisted.

"You do understand what she wants to do to you?" Durov asked incredulously.

Brie caressed her stomach. "Rytsar, I can't help but feel that what we do to her will follow us into the future. I want *moye solntse* to have a bright and promising future with nothing in our past to taint it."

"Wallace, I think you have presented us with a valid option," Thane said. "Do you mind working with Durov to find a suitable arrangement that will meet Brie's needs and ours?"

"Absolutely," he answered.

To Durov he said, "I look forward to working with you on this."

Durov grabbed Wallace by the hand and gave him a hearty handshake. "We will find the dog a new home far, far away."

To have the beginnings of a plan gave Thane solace. It would be something to hold onto as he fought against the dangerous rage that was building inside him.

Durov stood up. "I am going to visit the creature *now*."

"Not in your current state of mind, you're not," Thane told him emphatically.

The Russian slammed his fist on the table. "You cannot stop me, *moy droog*. My wrath must be satisfied."

"If you insist, then I will be forced to go with you."

Thane could not take the chance with Durov, but he loathed to see Lilly again.

"Will you take Brie back to the apartment?" he asked Mary.

Brie grabbed onto his arm. "But I want to stay with you."

"*Nyet, radost moya,*" Durov growled. "You will not go anywhere near her."

Brie looked up at Thane in desperation.

"Brie, it is my duty to make sure your wishes are honored concerning Lilly. I need you to trust me when I say you should go home now."

She stared at both men before falling to her knees and begging. "Please don't do anything to her."

Thane wheeled himself over to Durov, and placed his hand on him as reassurance, but noted that his friend was literally shaking with anger.

"We won't do anything rash," he told Brie. Then he turned to Durov, "Will we, old friend?"

Durov snarled but dutifully promised Brie, "I will not touch the creature."

"Thank you," she whispered.

Thane held out his hand, helping Brie back to her feet, wishing the nightmare that was Lilly was already a part of their past.

Brie put on a brave face for him, but pleaded, "Please, Sir, don't be gone long."

"I promise to be back as soon as possible."

She kissed him tenderly, and then went over to Durov. Thane noticed his friend visibly relax, when she put her hands on his chest and looked up at him.

The Russian let out an emotional sigh when she placed his hand on her belly. "All I ask is for you to keep *moye solntse's* future safe."

He kissed her on the forehead. "She will have a long and fruitful life—as will you, *radost moya*."

Brie smiled as she walked over to Wallace. "Thank you for coming up with a solution we can all live with."

He looked down at her, smiling warmly. "Funny, but I seem to see things more clearly with one eye."

She stared at his eye patch in admiration. "You truly are remarkable, Mr. Wallace."

"In a room of remarkable people," he answered.

"I've never forgotten the day we met—when you introduced yourself to me after saving me from the pavement."

"You saved me that day, as well, blossom. It was simply fate."

Brie grinned at him, nodding in agreement.

She turned her attention on Mary last.

"None of the mushy stuff for me, stinky," Mary warned her.

Brie laughed, and bumped her hip against Mary's. "You know I love you."

Mary scowled for a moment, before grabbing Brie and squeezing her tight. "Love you too, stinks."

Thane noticed Wallace staring at Mary intently and wondered what he was thinking. He requested Wallace stay behind after Brie and Mary left.

"I noticed you watching Miss Wilson just now. Is there a reason for that?"

"Although I realize that my plan for Lilly was a bust, there's been a real change in Mary. She's mentioned to Durov on several occasions that the survivor stories she's shared with Lilly have changed her outlook on life. And, today, she surprised me by opening up to Brie. You don't know what a huge step that was for her."

Thane nodded. "I have some idea. However, you're right, there's been a change."

"I'm glad Mary's finding her way."

"Enough of this jibber-jabber," Rytsar growled. "I have a date with the creature."

"Patience, old friend. I'm not leaving here until I know exactly what you have in mind."

"Just a simple tune whistled in the middle of the day when it's least expected."

"And that's it?" Thane pressed.

"I give you my solemn promise, comrade."

It was brilliant. Hearing Durov whistle that tune would strike a fear into Lilly's heart that nothing else could.

Thane smiled at both men as they left the room and headed down the hallway together.

It was a man's instinct to act—and to act fast. Anything less felt like chaos.

Before they went their separate ways, Thane stopped Wallace. "Never doubt your instincts. You've given Mary a new perspective, and you've given me clarity concerning Lilly's future."

Wallace nodded his appreciation and told Durov,

"Give her hell."

"Hellish nightmares," he agreed, letting out the roar of an angry lion ready to fight.

Thane appreciated that Durov had embraced his anger and found a way to express it.

Unfortunately, Thane did not have that ability. Lilly's threat to his family had set off his primal, protective side. But, with it, came his demons. He would need to keep his anger in check or be completely consumed by it.

Durov had told Brie he was not a monster, but Thane could not make that same claim. He knew that in the darkest part of his soul there lay a monster. All that was needed was the right catalyst, and those ominous whispers had begun their chant...

Thane couldn't sleep, consumed by thoughts of Lilly. He tried to leave the bed without waking Brie, but was clumsy in his transition from the bed to the wheelchair.

"What do you need, Sir? I can get it..." Brie mumbled in the dark.

"I don't need anything, babygirl. Go back to sleep."

Thane wheeled himself out of the room and headed to the living room, looking out the large window at the city before him. He stared at it blindly, too disturbed by the dark thoughts running through his head to be aware of what he saw.

After being confronted by the depths of Lilly's depravity, his desire for justice had morphed into something dark and repulsive. It went beyond a need to protect Brie and the baby, to something bordering on vicious.

These venomous thoughts and emotions were eating at him like cancer, and he feared that at some point he would either release them on Lilly or they would begin to eat him from the inside out.

The truth was, even though he said he didn't want to kill Lilly, he couldn't stop thinking about taking his revenge on her. For *every* act against Brie, the baby, and himself, Thane wanted to do an equally heinous act against her. He was certain she couldn't know his pain until she had suffered an equal share of it.

He didn't just want to get rid of Lilly, he wanted to make her suffer the way he had.

Maybe more.

Unconsciously hitting the arm of the chair repeatedly, Thane was so lost in his own inner battle that he failed to notice the creature creeping up on him until it was too late.

Thane cried out when the black beast landed on his lap. His reflexes took over and he flung the cat through the air before he even registered what it was.

The animal landed on its feet and sat down where it had fallen, staring at him.

"It wasn't personal," Thane told him.

The cat narrowed its eyes.

"You startled me. If anything, I should be upset with you. Why jump on me with no warning?"

Thane realized he was talking to the cat, and growled at himself in disgust. "I'm going insane, just like my mother. That's what this is."

He pressed his hands against his temples, a feeling of hopelessness washing over him. He had fought his demons ever since his father's death. He wasn't sure he had the strength to fight them any longer.

He felt the cat brush up against his leg. Thane dropped his hands and stared at the beast. "What do you want? I'm not the one who feeds you."

The cat sat on its haunches, looking as if he was preparing to jump.

When Thane didn't move, the animal took it as a sign of acceptance and leapt onto his lap.

Thane just stared at him, unsure what he was supposed to do. Like the tiny kitten at the hospital, the giant cat turned around several times, then lay down and began to purr.

Its purr seemed to radiate through Thane's body.

Thane shook his head.

This animal had pretty much ignored him since he'd come home from the hospital. He hadn't minded, since he wasn't exactly excited about owning a cat—but he owed the animal for his friend's life.

Luckily, the black tomcat was smart, keeping Brie company while staying out of his way. It was an agreeable arrangement.

Until tonight.

Thane looked down at him, unsure what this meant.

But its purr was soothing...

He placed a hand on the soft fur and the sound emanating from the animal increased, along with the vibration.

Thane took a deep breath and shut his eyes.

The physical presence of the cat seemed to calm his raging emotions and he could think again.

Thane opened his eyes, staring at the reflection of himself in the window.

The man before him was not a monster—just a man.

A normal, everyday man with a cat sitting on his lap.

He stroked the length of the animal with a new sense of appreciation.

"Shadow, I don't think I've formally introduced myself. My name is Thane, husband and Master to Brie."

The cat looked up at him briefly and twitched its tail before laying its head back down between its paws.

Thane stared at his reflection again, one thought running through his mind.

I determine my truth.

Mouse Ears

Thane had Brie drive them to the Italian café they'd often visited to enjoy cappuccinos together as a couple. He wanted to ensure, as much as possible, that these last few months before the baby was born were as normal and carefree as possible.

He was speaking with the owner, who had grown up on the same small island as his grandparents. While they were conversing about the recent changes taking place on Isola d' Elba, he noticed Brie staring out the window with a whimsical look on her face.

After he finished the conversation, he asked Brie, "What do you see out there that's caught your interest so?"

Brie eyes were sparkling. "There was a little girl walking past the café with her parents. She was so adorable, swinging in both their arms with Mickey Mouse ears on her head." Brie rested her chin against her hand, smiling at him. "The girl looked to be about the same age I was when I came to see Disneyland."

"I've never been, myself, but the expression on your

face lets me know you have good memories of it," he replied, taking a sip from his cup.

"Oh, I do, Sir!"

"How old were you?"

"Seven. My parents waited until I was old enough to remember the trip, but still young enough to believe in the magic."

Thane unconsciously did the calculations and felt a chill of providence course through him as he stared at Brie.

She blushed under his scrutiny. "What is it?"

"Tell me, babygirl, do you like Pluto?"

Brie laughed in delight. "I love Pluto! Is that something we have in common?"

Thane shook his head. "No, I have no preference in Disney characters, but I do remember a little girl who couldn't reach a bottle of catsup at a small diner Brad and I often frequented back in college."

Brie's jaw dropped. "Wait…"

Thane smirked. "She was a cute little thing, too. Long brown pigtails and a big smile. I recall that her father was none too pleased when she asked for my help to get that bottle for her."

She stared at him in shock. "Was that really you?"

He nodded.

"I've got goosebumps, Sir," Brie confessed, brushing her arm with her hand. She glanced at him shyly. "Did you know that you were my very first crush?"

"I was, was I?" he replied with a low growl.

"Of course! You were so handsome and kind." Brie blushed. "I confess I daydreamed about that college boy being my boyfriend for years."

Thane chuckled. "I've never forgotten how that man stared me down. I guess I have to give your father more credit. Somehow, he instinctually knew what I would be doing to his little girl someday."

Brie giggled.

Thane took her hand in his. "It seems we were fated for each other, my dear."

Tears came to her eyes as she nodded. "It really does, Sir."

Thane had a wild thought and asked, "What would you think if we sent your father Mickey Mouse ears and a bottle of catsup?"

Her eyes widened. "Oh, my goodness, that would be so funny!"

"Do you think he would remember?"

She grinned. "There's only one way to find out."

After weeks of contemplation, and being inspired by that fateful encounter, Brie announced she was finally ready to dole out her punishment.

He suggested they move to the sofa, and when she started to kneel, he explained, "It's better if you sit beside me. When punishing your Dominant, it's important that you are not in a submissive pose."

Brie blushed as she took a seat next to him on the couch. She began rubbing her hands on her knees nervously.

"There's no reason to feel anxious," he assured her, amused that she found the reversed power exchange uncomfortable.

Brie promptly stuck her hands between her knees to stop from fidgeting.

Thane waited patiently, but she just stared at him, her face growing redder by the moment as if she was afraid to declare his punishment aloud.

It was obvious Brie assumed whatever she had planned would displease him. Since he trusted Brie, and was determined to accept whatever she dished out, he knew he could handle it—no matter the level of discomfort.

"Go on," he encouraged her.

"I want to take you to a place you've never been."

"As in a mental challenge?" he asked, seeking clarification.

She grinned anxiously. "It will be, in a way."

"Very well. Tell me what I must do."

Brie took in a deep breath before she continued. "To pay homage to fate and my own childhood, I want you to take me to Disneyland."

Thane furrowed his brow. "I cannot physically complete that task, babygirl."

"But you can," she insisted, suddenly exuding confidence now that she had shared it with him. "We won't be going on the rides. We'll simply sit down at a restaurant to enjoy a meal together."

He could tell there was more involved and smirked knowingly. "What must I do? Wear a Mickey Mouse costume or perhaps your favorite—Pluto?"

Brie giggled, shaking her head. "I hadn't thought of that…"

"Then don't," he stated firmly, hoping he hadn't put a new idea in her head.

"The only thing required of you is to wave at the people, Sir."

"What?" Her answer had taken him completely by surprise.

"Ever since I rode on the Pirates of the Caribbean as a child, and I saw people waving at me from the restaurant by the river, I dreamed about being one of those people waving back."

Thane thought over what she'd shared before responding. "You realize this goes against my personality. I'm not a gregarious person."

Brie took his hand in both of hers. "I know, Sir. Hence the punishment aspect."

"So you want me waving at tourists?"

"No," she stated adamantly. "I want you waving at people who love the Disney experience. You will become part of their memories—forever."

"I have to hand it to you, Brie. This is *completely* out of my comfort zone."

"I know, Sir," she said in a solemn voice, "but I trust you will bear your punishment with a heart full of repentance."

Thane chuckled. "Do you have a sadistic streak, after all?"

Brie kept her solemn demeanor but he could see the doubt returning in her eyes. "You'll do it?"

"That was never a question."

Brie's smile returned. "Then this is going to be fun."

It was obvious in her excitement that she had forgotten the reason for the punishment, so he brought the conversation back to the heart of the issue. "I will complete your task because I broke a vital promise to you."

Brie fell back into her role and asked for more clarification. "What promise did you break, Sir?"

"I failed to be completely open with you. My desire to protect you is *not* a valid reason for breaking that vow."

Brie's expression changed, becoming more somber. "We cannot let anything stand between us—even silence."

Thane placed his hand on her stomach and looked at her with tender concern. "Agreed. We have too much at stake."

Brie kissed him on the lips. "I'll make the arrangements."

He was determined to honor her simple request. Considering the damage he'd unintentionally caused by keeping Lilly's threat from her, Thane appreciated that he was getting off relatively easy.

However, this punishment would be a challenge for him.

Thankfully, Brie only asked him to dress in a simple business suit—without the trademark ears—stating, "I want you to be humbled, Sir, nothing more."

"I appreciate that, Mrs. Davis,"

As she helped slip his jacket on, Thane took her hand and pulled her closer. "I'm highly tempted to bend you over my knee and spank that sexy bottom of yours purely for the enjoyment of it."

"That is a distinct possibility, Sir," she purred as she pulled away, quickly adding, "But only after your punishment."

It was enjoyable to watch Brie try to fulfill her role as the top in this situation, yet still fight the urge to please him as his submissive. It made her all that much more attractive.

"Your satisfaction is my primary goal tonight, téa."

Brie blushed in response to his declaration, kindling his Dominant desires further.

For her sake, Thane swallowed down the humiliation of having to be wheeled through the park by one of the Disney staff members as Brie walked beside him. He was used to being in a position of power, and everything about being in a wheelchair grated against his sensibilities.

Thane bore the indignity of children's curious stares, and the sympathetic glances of adults who recognized him as the crash victim/hero from the news, as they slowly made their way to the restaurant inside the park.

Looking at Brie, however, Thane was moved by how radiant she looked. Brie wore a set of Minnie Mouse ears with a red bow, her hair done up in pigtails. She even wore a flirtatious polka-dot dress reminiscent of the one she'd worn that day they'd met at the diner. Brie had done a magnificent job of capturing the look of his memory.

Knowing his duty was to take his punishment graciously made it slightly easier to bear when Brie took a seat, and the waiter pushed her chair in. That was his job as her Master.

Instead of being in control, Thane had to endure being pushed up to the table like a child. The man even laid his napkin on his lap, saying, "There you go, Mr. Davis. Enjoy your meal."

Thane nodded to the man, but felt the eyes of others on him, and had to shake the feeling of mortification it inspired. This was not about him, or his inabilities, but the beautiful woman sitting across the table—and rectifying his mistake.

"Do you like it, Sir?" Brie asked excitedly, staring at the manmade river lazily flowing beside the restaurant.

The establishment itself was dark, as if they were sitting outside on a veranda. The sound of crickets and frogs playing in the background blended with a night sky illuminated above them.

"It's quite unique," he answered truthfully, impressed by the re-creation.

The waiter returned with a basket of rolls. Turning to Thane, he asked, "What would you like to drink?"

Brie piped up, "Sir, I googled this place and thoroughly studied the menu."

Thane smiled. "Of course you did, my dear. Why don't you order drinks for both of us?"

When the man returned with their drinks, Brie squealed in delight. "Look, the ice cubes really do glow in the dark."

Thane held up his mint julep and stared at it with an amused smirk. "I can't say I've ever had a drink that glowed."

Brie suddenly set her glass down as an adorable look came over her face and Thane was reminded of that little girl years ago. Brie cried out, "Look, Sir. It's our first boat!"

She started waving wildly at the people on the Pirates of the Caribbean ride.

A few boat riders waved back hesitantly. Thane looked around the restaurant and noticed Brie was the only diner waving. Understanding his role tonight, he lifted his hand and smiled as he joined Brie in waving at the people.

Even more boat riders responded, causing Brie to giggle in delight.

Seeing both of them greeting the boat riders inspired those around them to do the same. Soon half the diners were waving along with Brie, making those on the boat ride more animated and vocal.

When Brie glanced at him, her eyes were sparkling. "Sir, I just love this! It's even more wonderful than I imagined."

As the evening wore on, Thane noticed that every time Brie was about to take a bite from her plate, a new boat would float past. She instantly forgot about eating, putting her fork down to wave and say hello to anyone who drifted past.

Thane did not want his submissive to leave the restaurant hungry, so he fed her small bites between each boat that floated past. Seeing Brie so carefree moved him deeply. Despite all that had happened, she still held the childlike wonder and vitality that had attracted him to her.

A little boy yelled from a boat, "Throw a roll!"

Brie looked at Thane, lamenting, "I can't aim worth anything."

"Come on, please…" the kid begged as he slowly drifted past.

Without hesitation, Thane picked up one of the rolls in the basket, calculated the distance, and threw it into the boy's open hands.

"Thank you, mister!" he cried, before taking a big bite.

Thane smiled and waved at him as if it was a perfectly natural thing to do.

When he looked back at Brie, Thane found her staring at him with tears in her eyes.

"What?" he chuckled.

"I don't think I could love you more than I do right now." Brie got up from her seat and walked over to him. She gave him a gentle kiss on the lips, but followed it up with a longer, more passionate one.

Again, Thane could feel all eyes on them, but this time he didn't mind. Reaching up, he clasped her behind the neck and gave her a kiss she would not forget.

She stumbled back to her seat, staring at him amorously from across the table.

He felt humbled and intensely grateful to be here now. Somehow, by the grace of God, he'd survived the crash so that this moment could be part of his reality.

Thane looked upward and mouthed two words, "Thank you."

He sat with her and waved for another hour, in no hurry to rush when it was obvious how much she was enjoying herself. Afterward, he paid the waiter a generous tip for the extra time and asked the staff member who had helped him if he would take them to a gift shop on their way out.

"Are you getting a pair of ears to remember this night?" Brie asked as he studied the wide assortment of mouse ears.

"Ah, no. I'm actually getting a pair for your father."

Brie broke out in a peal of laughter. "You're really going through with it, huh?"

"What kind of son would I be if I forgot my parents at a time like this? Tell me, what do you think your mother would like?"

Brie looked at a glass counter and pointed to a Bambi music box with a butterfly on his tail. "She would love this."

Thane looked up at the cashier. "Would you mind adding that, as well? Oh, and that stuffed animal over there."

"Which one?" the cashier asked.

"The yellow dog."

"Oh, you mean Pluto?"

"Yes. I happen to know someone who 'just loves Pluto'." He glanced over at Brie and winked at her.

When the young cashier tried to stuff Pluto into the plastic bag, Brie quickly intervened. "Pluto needs to be carried."

The cashier smiled at Thane. "Guess I found your Pluto lover."

"Indeed."

They were almost out of the store when Thane spotted something on the far wall and asked to return to the cashier.

"I have one more purchase."

"Certainly. What can I get for you?"

Thane smiled as he pointed at the display on the wall.

She walked over and picked up a pull-along baby Pluto and complimented him as she rang it up. "Excellent choice, sir."

Brie made a cute little squeak beside him.

Thane told the cashier, "I have a sneaking suspicion our child will be a Pluto fan, as well."

Brie suddenly accosted Thane, wrapping her arms around him and kissing him repeatedly. Before she pulled away, she whispered, "I forgive you, Sir."

Thane took her hand and kissed it. "Thank you, Mrs. Davis."

Once they arrived home, he reasserted his role as her Master—free from the guilt that had plagued him.

"Strip off those panties, little girl. This college boy is about to pinken that fine ass…"

Honey

"I have met the most wonderful nun, comrade!"

Thane was aware that Durov and Wallace had located a situation. One that they felt could provide the solution they were seeking with Lilly. It was so promising that Durov had even postponed his operation so the two could travel there to assess it personally. After a lengthy trip, they had come back ready to share their findings with Thane.

But that statement was the last thing Thane ever expected to hear from Durov's lips. The man was not known to be religious or to have a fetish for nuns. "Really?"

"*Da*, Mother Yana is perfection," Durov exclaimed proudly.

Knowing the Russian was a jokester, he turned to Wallace. "Is he pulling my leg?"

"I wouldn't be here if he was."

Thane studied Durov warily, still not convinced.

"Yana is the most uncompromising woman I have ever met, *moy droog*. She does not believe in rest or comfort, only service."

"Service to whom?"

"To God, of course, and to the poor among us."

Wallace added, "The Reverend Mother is interested in Lilly. Actually, more than just interested. She feels a calling to take Lilly under her care."

Thane shot a glance at Durov. "I expected you would find something more punitive for her."

Durov grinned. "You have not met the esteemed Mother Yana. Even *I* am intimidated by the woman."

"Forgive my skepticism, but a nunnery?"

Wallace explained, "The Reverend Mother believes in redemption of the lost. She has built her life around the conviction that hard work and physical sacrifice is the first step on that path. Lilly would rise before dawn every morning, say prayers with the sisters, and work in the garden for the sole purpose of feeding the poor. When not in the garden, she would serve the needs of the abbey until it was time for bed. The Reverend Mother is convinced idle time is the devil's work."

"And if Lilly refuses?" Thane scoffed.

"There will be swift, physical punishment. The Reverend Mother does not tolerate disobedience. She said that the body must be subdued, and thoughts silenced before a soul can hear God. It has been the focus of the convent for decades to help the condemned souls of their society by providing this path to salvation."

Durov laughed. "Since I am convinced the creature has no soul, I foresee her slaving to feed the poor until her dying breath. I will get the punishment I seek, and *radost moya* will get the assurance that her babe's future carries no taint, because not only will the creature's life be spared, but she will be making a positive difference to the world—whether she wants to or not."

"But you know how shrewd Lilly is. What's going to stop her from manipulating this woman?"

Durov answered, "Mother Yana is uncommonly perceptive, to the point of being unnerving."

"Much like Marquis Gray," Wallace explained. "Both Durov and I were extremely impressed by the Reverend Mother, Sir Davis, as well as her desire to work with the unredeemable."

"Do you actually believe she could have an influence over Lilly?"

Wallace shook his head. "No, not after what happened here. But Lilly will be treated fairly in an environment that will ensure Brie's continued safety."

"How can you be sure of that?"

"*Moy droog*," Durov answered, "this convent is located in a very remote village. So isolated that there are no roads to it. It took us days to get there with help. The creature will come to the convent literally as naked as the day she was born—no passport, no clothes and no means of escape."

"Unless she enlists help from an outside source."

Durov chuckled. "*Nyet,* comrade. They mark the unredeemed so that no one will touch them."

Thane frowned. "What kind of marking?"

"The nuns shave their heads."

Thane felt a stirring of hope. "That's perfect for her. A physical reminder for Lilly of what she had done, while also acting as a warning to others."

"*Da*," Durov agreed with great satisfaction.

"If this convent is so remote, how did you find out about it?"

"Titov." Durov spoke the man's name with great affection. "Even though he no longer works for me, he still proves invaluable. Better still, he has begun his quest for a family."

"Starting so soon?" Wallace asked with amusement.

"Titov is determined like *moy droog*. I was told his first will be gracing the world in seven months' time." He added with a smirk, "I suggested the name Alexei, and should they turn out to have twins, Nikodim for the second."

"Naming other people's children now?" Thane teased.

He replied with a grin, "Titov and I have an under-standing."

Thane knew there were aspects of Durov's life he would never be privy to. The long and complicated relationship with Titov was one of them. Ever since he'd first met Durov in college, the Russian had been vague about the history the two men shared. Thane knew he was Tatianna's brother and that Durov had blamed him initially for her capture. The Russian never said why that changed or why Titov felt the need to work with Durov all these years.

He suspected that something significant had happened between them in Russia the year after the murder of Durov's mother. Whatever that was, it had had the power to connect them together for life.

Thane admired the devotion that Durov inspired in

people—himself included. The pure passion of the man was infectious, and his courage was undisputable. However, that was not what Thane admired most. He knew the sensitive soul that resided under the gruff exterior that Durov presented to the world. That part he only trusted with a very select few.

"I digress, comrade. This discussion is not about Titov or his little *rebenok*. Both Wallace and I feel confident about this choice of Mother Yana. What are your thoughts?"

The fact that Durov approved, a man who understood Thane's need to permanently eliminate Lilly as a threat, was extremely important to Thane. With Wallace on board as well, he felt certain that Brie would agree.

"If she agrees, comrade, we will make the transfer after I have recovered sufficiently from my surgery to travel there," Durov said.

"It can be done without you," Thane assured him.

"*Nyet*. It must be you and me, brother. *We* need to deliver the creature to her fate."

All of Thane's hard work with physical therapy was beginning to pay off. He was now able to walk with the aid of a cane. It meant he could join Brie on normal, everyday activities like a simple trip to the grocery store. He felt a deep sense of pride as he walked upright beside his woman, fully independent. It was a small but meaningful victory.

While Brie was picking out apples from the bin, Thane noticed a dark-haired man staring at her. When the man realized he'd been noticed, he nodded to Thane and moved on.

"It appears you have another admirer, my dear."

Brie giggled, clutching her stomach. "When I'm eight months pregnant? I don't think so."

Thane tilted her chin up and kissed her. "You're beautiful. Of course, men can't help but notice."

Her eyes sparkled with amusement. "That's hard to believe when I feel like an overweight duck the way I have to waddle these days."

Thane fisted her hair and pulled her head back. "You're *my* sexy pregnant woman." He kissed her hard, expressing his adoration with his tongue.

Brie grabbed onto the cart for balance afterward. "Your kisses…they still make me weak."

"I think it would be best if I take you home now," he growled lustfully. "That kiss has inspired me."

As they were leaving the store, Brie stopped in her tracks. "Oh no, I forgot the honey."

"Can't it wait?"

She smiled up at him amorously, licking her lips. "No, husband. It's *very* important. Do you mind if I go back and get it?"

Her ardent gaze had him intrigued. "Certainly, baby-girl. Get it while I load up the car."

As Thane was putting the last bag into the trunk, he looked up to see the same man standing by the doors at the entrance, watching Brie as she came out. Brie's gaze was locked on Thane as she held up her container of honey and grinned at him, completely unaware of the man beside her.

Thane's hackles went up and he started walking toward her as quickly as he could, leaning heavily on the cane. "Brie, come here," he commanded loudly, wanting the man to know he was aware of him. The sound of his voice caused the man to glance in Thane's direction. As soon as their eyes met, he quickly turned and walked the other way.

Thane grabbed Brie around the shoulders and guided her to the car.

"Is everything okay, Sir?" she asked, picking up on his uneasiness.

Although the man hadn't made a move toward Brie, the intense way he had stared at her deeply disturbed Thane.

"I'd like to take a detour to Durov's," he replied. "The same man who was watching you in the store was waiting outside when you came out."

She looked surprised. "I didn't even notice."

"I'm probably being paranoid, but I didn't like the way he was staring at you."

Brie shuddered.

"Don't worry, babygirl. I'm always looking out for you."

Brie wrapped her arms around Thane, her round belly pressing hard against him. It filled him with an overwhelming sense of responsibility and a need to protect. The darkness that had been lying in wait now reared its ugly head, ready to do battle.

"I don't mind taking a detour to the beach house, Sir.

I like any excuse to visit Rytsar."

Durov and his dog, Little Sparrow, were waiting at the door when they arrived. He held out his hands to Brie. "Little mama, come to your Russian."

Brie ran into his embrace, smiling at Sir as he hugged her in his beefy arms. With time, Durov was beginning to fill out and look more like the burly Russian they knew.

Thane appreciated the look of pure joy on Durov's face. In all the years he'd known the man, he'd never seen his friend this content. Knowing what Durov had been through in his life, it was proof that life was worth holding onto, no matter how bleak things became.

Durov held out his hand to Thane while still holding onto Brie. "Good to see you again, brother. What brings you here so unexpectedly?"

Thane hated to cut short his bliss, but told him, "As I mentioned to Brie, it's possible I'm being overly protective, but I wanted to share what happened at the grocery store just now."

Durov spread his arm wide, gesturing him into the house. "Please come in and tell me all about the giant cucumber you two were ogling."

Brie giggled as they all went inside.

The little pup jumped around excitedly, wagging her tail as the three made their way to the couch. It was obvious the animal was ecstatic to have visitors. When they sat down, Little Sparrow walked over to Brie and licked her hand enthusiastically. She then went to Thane and nudged her head under his hand. The dog wagged her tail when Thane petted her. After greeting them both, she settled at Durov's feet, sitting at attention looking at them both.

Durov became serious when he asked Thane, "What is bothering you, comrade?"

"Be honest if you believe this is nothing. I feel like a raging bull right now."

"What is it?" Durov asked, now sounding concerned.

"I noticed a man looking Brie over as we were shopping today."

"That is not unusual, *moy droog*," Durov stated, winking at Brie.

"I saw him again, waiting by the entrance, when she came out of the store while I was busy loading groceries into the car. Durov, he seemed very intent on her."

Durov's sudden frown alarmed him. "What did he look like?"

"Dark hair, brown eyes—possibly Arabian descent. Why do you ask?"

Durov shot a glance at Brie, now clearly troubled. "I will have two of my men by your side at all times, *radost moya*."

Turning to Thane, he said, "You were right to be concerned. I suspect the creature must not have returned the money she took when she sold Brie but failed to deliver. The man must have sent someone to collect his purchase."

"The slaver?" Thane felt his pulse race. "But Brie's about to give birth. Why would he want her now?"

"She carries a baby *girl*," Durov stated ominously.

"What would he do with our child?" Brie cried.

Durov's voice grew cold. "I have seen it before. The

man would either keep *moye solntse* for himself or sell the babe to the highest bidder."

Brie shook her head, looking at Sir in horror.

Thane embraced her, squeezing Brie hard against his chest, his rage threatening to explode. "I should have trusted my instincts and called the police or, at the very least, confronted the man myself."

"*Nyet*. Your keen eye and intuition has given us the upper hand. I'll have my men start combing the streets. We will find out who he is and who he works for."

"We will *make* Lilly tell us," Thane growled, ready to head out the door.

Durov stopped him. "I already asked her while she was under my charge, comrade. I wanted to 'take care' of him so that no other woman would have to suffer. But this purchase was done on the dark web through an anonymous third party. The creature does not know who it is, I am sure of it."

Brie shuddered in Thane's arms, and he held her even tighter. "I won't let anything happen to you, Brie."

Durov added his assurance. "*Radost moya*, no one will lay a hand on you." He called out to his men, assigning two to watch over Brie, and the others to seek out his contacts around town.

"We will find out what we need to know," he assured Thane.

Brie stood up and addressed the two men assigned to guard her. "Thank you for your help."

One cleared his throat. "It is our duty." He looked at Durov before adding.

"As well as our pleasure to do so, Mrs. Davis."

Durov dropped to one knee and spoke to Brie's stomach. "Your *dyadya* is here. I am counting the days until we meet, tiny one." He kissed her round tummy before standing up.

Addressing Thane, he said, "It would be good if the two of you stayed here." He paused, his eyes revealing his unease. "I could use the distraction."

"I'm afraid we can't," Thane answered with regret, knowing his friend would be disappointed. "My physical therapist is not able to change his schedule and, with this new threat looming, I can't waste even a day."

Brie looked out the huge bay window, ignoring both men as she stared at the ocean. She said in a sad, wistful voice, "I have always found the ocean soothing."

Thane looked at Durov, nodding to him, the two understanding what she needed.

Walking over to her, Thane put his arm around her waist. "There's no reason we can't stay here for the afternoon."

Durov moved to her other side. "I hear the waters are particularly warm today. Would you like to take a dip?"

Since Brie did not have a swimsuit, Durov gave her a set of his boxers with a stretchy waistband and a white tee shirt that fit snuggly around her belly. She looked into the mirror and laughed at herself. "I'm a hot mess."

Rytsar stood behind her admiring his handiwork. "Not so, *radost moya*. When that shirt gets wet, you will look very charming."

She turned her head toward him. "Going for the wet tee shirt contest look, are you?"

He reached around and grabbed her breasts in both hands. "These fine beauties should never be covered, but you Americans have prudish laws."

She giggled as she glanced over at Thane. "You look sexy in Rytsar's swim trucks, by the way."

Pulling down on the yellow shorts, Thane grumbled, "I'm not used to wearing micro shorts and calling them swimwear."

"We Russians are not ashamed of our bodies," Durov chuckled, showing off the skintight red ones he sported, which emphasized his frontal assets. He turned and flexed his buttocks for her. "You would miss out on this if I wore the oversized pajamas you normally wear."

"At least our swimwear is comfortable," Thane stated.

Durov spread his arms wide. "I *am* comfortable."

"And horny." Thane raised an eyebrow. "Because there's no hiding it in these."

"Why would I want to hide it? I want *radost moya* to know what I'm thinking," he said, giving her a wink.

Brie giggled again. Thane was grateful for Durov's ability to help her focus on other things. He was determined to do the same, letting the tranquility of the ocean take over for this brief moment in time.

The cane was useless in the sand, so Thane leaned on Durov to make it to the water's edge, but once in the ocean, he was suddenly free of gravity as he floated in the current. It was a miraculous feeling.

He looked at Brie and saw she shared a similar look of wonder as she laughed in delight. "Look at me—I'm light as a feather. I'm free!"

Brie was facing Thane when she said it and didn't see the large wave advancing on her.

"Brie!" he called out, but was too late. He watched her head disappear under the water. Thane felt a moment of panic as he and Durov swam toward her, but she popped back up, spitting out water and laughing.

"Are you okay?" he asked when he reached her.

"The ocean is just having fun." Brie turned to face the next wave and shook a finger at it. "You naughty ocean, trying to have your way with me…"

Thane grabbed her and pulled her to him, the two floating together effortlessly in the water. Brie sighed against him.

"This is wonderful, Sir. Makes me feel like a kid again—a kid who doesn't have a giant belly and weighs a gazillion pounds."

"I know what you mean. I haven't felt this physically free in a long time." He handed Brie over to Durov and took off swimming just to prove to himself he could.

The three of them spent hours floating on the waves, forgetting the world existed. Their bliss continued when they returned to the beach house. The men took turns lathering Brie up and rinsing her off so she was completely free of sand.

When she stepped into the bedroom, clean and dry, Durov growled huskily, "You know what I do with cunts? I eat them. Now drop that towel and lie on the bed."

Brie giggled as Durov led her to the bed and promptly buried his head between her legs. Thane lay on the bed beside her and sampled her breasts, knowing that the right amount of suction would intensify her orgasm.

Within a matter of minutes, Brie was crying out, "Oh yes, oohhh, God, yes!" as she came.

Durov looked up from her round belly and smiled at Thane. "She is so hot these days."

"I've noticed that myself."

"What shall we do now, *moy droog?*"

"I have an idea," Brie piped up. "You know that honey I wanted?" She gave Thane an innocent smile. "I'd like to show you why I bought it."

Thane glanced at Durov. "Are you up for us making a mess of your bed?"

The Russian answered by lifting Brie up off the bed and pulling the covers off. "*Da.* And, afterward, I have a surprise of my own."

Thane slipped on his pants and grabbed his cane, heading out to get the honey from the car. He heard the sounds of the rolling waves as he unlocked the car and stopped for a moment. It astounded him how much this simple trip to the beach had relaxed his warring spirit. The call of the waves was like a song, soothing the savage beast within him.

He understood better why Durov insisted on living here whenever he was in LA, and toyed with the idea of selling his apartment for beachfront property.

With the honey in hand, Thane returned to the house and asked Brie, "What is your plan for this, babygirl?"

"I need two naked men on the bed. I plan to tease you with this succulent nectar. I saw it done on a video and it looked yummy."

"Don't tell me—you googled it."

"Of course, Sir! Isn't that what every good sub does?"

Durov lay on the bed first, stroking his already rigid cock. "Do you want it like this?" he asked, holding his shaft straight up to show off its length.

"Yes, Rytsar. That's perfect."

Thane lay down on the other side of the bed, his cock already standing at attention.

Brie put her damp hair into a ponytail, warning them, "This could get messy."

Climbing onto the bed, Brie grasped Thane's cock first and smiled at him as she tipped the plastic honey bottle, squeezing it just enough so that a thin stream came out. She swirled it around his cock, starting at the balls and slowly swirling all the way up until it ringed the head of his shaft.

She handed the bottle to Durov before lowering those luscious lips onto Thane's cock, licking his shaft like a lollipop before going down on him and sucking the honey. She stopped midway and left him in that state as she moved to Durov and took the bottle from him, repeating the process.

The Russian groaned lustfully in pleasure but complained when she stopped to return to Thane.

"I have to play fair, Rytsar." Leaning forward, she gave him a sticky kiss. The Russian grunted his displeasure as she left him for Thane.

Thane smiled at Durov as those warm lips encased his shaft, and he groaned in ecstasy as she sucked, nibbled, and licked his entire shaft until it was clean and ready for her grand finale.

Brie switched things up by looking at Durov, instead of him, as she took Thane deep into her throat and began to bob up and down on his shaft. She continued until the urge became too great and he grabbed her head, feeding her his orgasm.

She moaned, licking his spent shaft before moving to Durov.

The Russian was desperate for her attention and immediately pushed her mouth down onto his cock.

Thane watched as she slowly and sensually took control, licking his balls first before sucking them into her mouth and moaning. Durov visibly shuddered. She then licked and nibbled up the base of his shaft, cleaning him off until he was ready for his own finale.

Brie's gaze met Thane's as she slowly took the length of Durov's shaft down her throat. She made it look hot as hell, a far cry from her earlier days. When she began bobbing her head up and down, Thane felt his cock stir again, wanting more of that talented mouth.

Durov did not last long. Fisting Brie's curls, he let out a spirited roar as he orgasmed in her mouth. Afterward, he lay there like a dead man with a satisfied smile on his face.

Brie lay between them, her face sticky from her efforts, and smiled at Thane. "I like honey."

Thane chuckled, leaning over to kiss her sticky cheek. "I must confess, I have an appreciation for it myself."

The three of them lay there satiated and happy as they listened to the rolling waves outside. Thane relished this feeling of bliss and allowed himself to just be...

After a while, Durov stirred and left the bed. "Get her cleaned up, *moy droog*, while I get her surprise."

Thane took Brie's hand and helped her up, curious about what Durov had in mind. After she washed herself up, he undid the band in her hair and took time to brush out her silky brown curls. She tilted her head back, goosebumps covering her shoulders as she purred, "Sir, that feels *so* good…"

Thane smiled, relishing the simple but intimate exchange between them. When Durov announced he was ready, Thane escorted her out and presented her to him.

The man stood before them with his hands behind his back. "Are you ready to have your mind blown, *radost moya?*"

She smiled nervously. "Sure…"

He raised an eyebrow.

"Yes, Rytsar," she answered with a bow, adding, "Please."

He smiled broadly as he revealed what was hidden in his right hand. Durov tossed a length of rope to Thane. "You will tie her up."

Brie grinned, shivering in anticipation.

Durov then showed what he was hiding in his left hand. "I will be the one to insert this." It was a small silicone device, only two and a half inches long, with a flared base on one end and a curved tip on the other. It had the circumference of a thick shaft. Thane suspected it was a vibrator, but hadn't seen one like it before.

Brie stared at it, her eyes flashing with excitement. "What does it do, Rytsar?"

He only smirked in answer and told Thane, "It was

given the green light by her doctor."

Thane appreciated that Durov was being careful when it came to playing with Brie during her pregnancy.

Setting the device on the nightstand, Durov kissed Brie passionately as he pushed her onto the bed. He then gestured to Thane to join him while he nibbled her neck.

The two took turns sucking and biting as they explored her body with their hands and teeth. Brie wiggled and moaned in pleasure, responding favorably to the attention of both men.

Durov reached between her legs and grunted in satisfaction. "She is wet and hungry for it." Brie whimpered as he took the unknown instrument from the nightstand and asked her to spread her legs for him.

He chuckled, commenting to Thane, "She is going to love this."

"When do I tie her," he asked, holding up the rope.

"Soon, *moy droog.*"

Durov lay beside her and looked deep into her eyes as he slowly penetrated her pussy with the device. Brie bit her lip, keeping eye contact with him, but Thane noticed she was breathing much more rapidly.

Once it was inserted, Durov bit down on the sensitive area of her neck before moving away.

"Tie her legs together from her thighs to her ankles, brother. Make it tight."

Brie smiled as Thane took over, sliding the rope over her skin with each pass, seducing her with the soft nylon cord as he kissed her after tying each knot.

Moaning softly in response, Brie gave into the binding, whispering "Thank you" when he was finished. Brie lay there completely helpless on the bed with the mysterious instrument inside her.

Her eyes returned to Rytsar, filled with curiosity and a hint of fear.

"Kiss her, *moy droog*."

Thane lay down beside her and tasted her mouth, dancing his tongue over her lips before plundering it deeply.

Durov moved up behind to spoon her. Wrapping his arm around her waist, he growled lustfully, "Relax…"

Brie immediately tensed as the low sound of a vibrator emanated from inside her. She moaned into Sir's mouth, her kisses quickly becoming more passionate and aggressive.

"She likes it," Thane told him.

Durov grabbed one of her breasts and lowered his head to suck on it, stating confidently, "I knew she would."

Soon Brie was squirming, her cries of passion growing louder. "It's so intense! Oh, my God, it's so intense."

Her sexual excitement spurred Thane's own as he watched her body shuddering in an orgasm. She was gasping for breath when the next one crashed over her.

"Ohhh," she moaned as another hit immediately after. The little vibrator Durov had found was obviously stimulating her G-spot in a way that was coaxing continuous climaxes, and Brie was helpless to stop them. The bondage, along with the mysterious toy, sent his beautiful wife into subspace.

Thane was entranced as he watched her take flight. Whispering in her ear, he told Brie, "How I love watching you fly, babygirl…"

Justice

Durov called to inform Thane that a man fitting the same description he had given was caught on the surveillance tape just outside the TLC.

"We have to meet."

"Agreed, comrade."

"I'll call Wallace and see if we can have it as his place for convenience."

"Just tell me the time and place and I will be there. We don't have a minute to lose."

"Understood."

Thane's heart began racing. This unknown threat had the potential of destroying everything he held dear.

When the three met, the first thing out of Thane's mouth was, "What the hell is he doing at Stephanie's center?"

Wallace answered him first. "I'm afraid the buyer suspects Lilly is there and is seeking payment."

"But how is that possible? How could he know?"

"I have no idea, comrade," Durov answered, "but the situation has now become volatile."

"Do you know who he is?" Thane demanded.

"We do not have a name yet, but I have confirmed he left the country shortly after casing the center last night."

"Do you think he left to report back to his employer?" Wallace asked Durov.

"I can only assume. In my opinion, the fact that he went in search of her is fortunate. I suspect the buyer was verifying Brie's location so that he could reclaim his investment from the creature. But, being that she is penniless and unable to pay, her life is forfeit."

"You believe they plan to kill her?"

"It would be an easy fix for us to do nothing, but we cannot endanger the girls at the center, or risk something happening to Miss Wilson. We must act now."

"Agreed," Wallace said. "With Lilly's location compromised, we need to get her out before he returns, and erase all evidence she was ever there."

Thane turned to Durov. "But your surgery is this week."

"I've already postponed it. You and I must do this together, brother," he stated emphatically.

"How soon do you think we can leave?" Thane asked.

"I will need to set up a meeting place and transportation, and arrange the transfer. It may take me a day or two."

"The sooner the better," Wallace insisted.

"Agreed."

Thane was still worried about Brie's safety, even with Durov's men guarding her. Until the man was identified and his motivations known, he would remain a serious threat.

Turning to Wallace, Thane asked, "Would you look after Brie? I need to know she's protected."

Thane could see the fear in Brie's eyes when he told her that he was going to transport Lilly to the convent with Durov.

"Can't I go with you, Sir?"

"Absolutely not. Your health, and that of the baby's, is paramount."

Brie said nothing, but she was physically shaking when he wrapped his arms around her. "Nothing is going to happen," he promised. "Durov has it planned out—every detail and contingency."

Despite his assurances, tears filled her eyes. "I can't stay behind. I'll go crazy if I do."

To relieve her fears—and his—Thane had found something that would help them both during this unwanted separation.

He placed her hand on his chest so Brie could feel his heartbeat.

Thane ordered her to look at him. When her honey-colored eyes met his, he felt her beginning to relax.

"I can't have you going crazy."

"No, Sir."

"But I have to take care of this."

"I know," she said in the barest of whispers, her bottom lip trembling. "It's just that—"

He put his finger to her lips, finishing her sentence. "You lost me once and you don't want to lose me again."

Tears rolled down her cheeks as she nodded.

"I understand, and I feel the same way, babygirl. That's why I got us a gift of sorts." Thane walked over to his desk and opened the middle drawer, pulling out two ring boxes. He gestured to her to sit on the couch with him so he could explain what they were.

Handing Brie the smaller box, he asked her to open it.

She lifted the lid and looked at the black ring edged in silver nestled inside. She looked up at him tenderly. "It's beautiful, Sir."

He took it out of the box and explained, "It is also practical." Sliding it onto her finger, he said, "Wherever we are, whatever we're doing, we will be able to feel each other's heartbeat."

She looked at him questioningly as he put on his own ring.

"All you have to do is tap on the ring once like this." He tapped his index finger on her ring and waited to see her reaction.

After several seconds, her eyes lit up with joy. "I can feel it!" When it ended, she smiled at him. Placing her hand on Thane's chest, she asked him to tap it again.

This time she looked at him in wonder. "I can really feel your heartbeat, Sir."

Thane tapped his own ring and felt the steady beat of Brie's heart pulsing on his finger. "We will always be connected, no matter how far apart."

She shook her head in disbelief, staring at the ring in awe. "This is truly the most precious gift you could have gotten me."

He placed his hand on her stomach. "This is the most precious gift you could give me."

Brie placed her hand on his and sighed with contentment. "You are going to make a wonderful father."

He had his reservations, but remained determined to follow in his father's footsteps, letting Alonzo's loving nature guide him rather than his mother's dark demons.

Smiling down at Brie, he asked, "Will you be able to let me leave now?"

Brie frowned for a moment, but tapped her ring and closed her eyes as she waited. A smile spread across her lips as she opened her eyes.

He leaned over and kissed her. "So, we're good?"

She pressed her ear against his chest and tapped her ring again. Her smile returned. "Yes, Sir."

He wrapped his arms around her, grateful for technology that allowed them both a meaningful way to stay connected while apart. He felt certain it would be a long time before either of them was comfortable taking them off.

Durov and Thane came to Lilly in the night, having told Mary her services were no longer needed.

It seemed to Thane that Lilly was on alert because of

Mary's unexplained absence. She cried out to them as they approached her door. "What's happening? Where's my friend? I demand to know!"

They stopped in front of the door and Durov whistled his simple tune.

Lilly began screaming hysterically.

Thane opened the door and walked in alone. As soon as she saw him, she stopped her hysterics. "Oh, my God, Thane! You about scared the crap out of me." She laughed nervously, smiling at him. "I can't tell you how glad I am to see you right now."

He stepped aside to allow Durov to enter the room. Thane took great satisfaction in watching the color drain from her face.

"I am here to finish the job," Durov stated in his thick Russian accent.

Lilly looked at Thane with wild desperation. "Don't let him near me, Thane. I'm your sister. You know I love you."

His fury was rising to dangerous levels just being in her presence. It was taking everything in Thane not to kill her with his bare hands—this woman who had not only hurt Brie, but had also threatened to kill their unborn child.

"Gag her," he spat, not trusting himself to touch her.

The Russian was swift, pulling Lilly to her feet, the sound of the rattling chain echoing in the room. He taped her mouth before she could protest, then released her from the metal collar. Wrapping his hand around her throat, he told Thane, "I could snap it."

Lilly's eyes grew wide, her terror palpable, as her

muffled screams filled Thane's ears. He wasn't sure if Durov was jesting or if he meant it. His need for justice demanded she pay for her crimes against his family, but Thane resisted the urge to end it here.

He knew why he'd come and where his loyalties lay. He would give Brie exactly what she had asked for, whether this woman before him deserved it or not.

Thane pulled a syringe from his pocket. With cold determination, he approached her and thrust the needle into her arm, taking pleasure in the sound of her muffled cries. When she stopped struggling and fell limp in Durov's arms, Thane growled, "Let's get this over with."

The Russian picked her up, grunting in pain but smiling just the same. "It feels good to give her a taste of her own medicine, does it not?"

"A little too good," Thane agreed, unsettled by the blind hatred he felt toward Lilly. He could no longer see her humanity, only the threat she posed to his family. The fact that they were related made him hate her even more. Thane pressed the ring on his finger and felt Brie's steady heartbeat. The feel of it acted like a homing beacon, reminding him who he was and where he belonged beyond this dark rage boiling inside him.

They kept Lilly sedated the entire plane trip to Russia, neither man being in the right frame of mind to interact with her. Instead, the two spent their time playing chess against each other just as they had in their college days.

It provided a healthy distraction for Thane whenever his mind wandered to darker places.

It seemed to Thane that Durov had improved greatly

since the last time they played, and he found himself struggling to counter his friend's attacks. "Have you been taking lessons?"

"*Nyet*, but I see that you are distracted," Durov replied, his tone serious. "I know you struggle and fear that the rage inside is changing you. Do not fret, *moy droog*. You are still the same man. We determine our truth. No one else—not the world, not our circumstances, and not those around us. *We* are in control."

Thane looked at him and shook his head, those words being familiar to him. "Using my own words against me?"

"*Nyet*, comrade. You spoke a deep truth after my mother's death. It has stuck with me these many years. These feelings boiling up inside you and clouding your mind are temporary. You will find a way through them."

Thane glanced at where Lilly was sleeping. "Being near her brings out the worst in me."

Durov put his hand on Thane's shoulder. "We do this together, to keep each other in check. We will deliver her as we have promised."

"Would you really have broken her neck?"

"You had only to say the word, and I would have."

Thane sighed. "You and I are dangerous together."

Durov disagreed. "It is natural we should want to act against those who seek to harm us. We are behaving the way we were designed—as protectors. It is your woman who is forcing us to change our natural course. Even though I was violently against it, I agree with *radost moya* now. Your babe deserves a future free of sins from the past. That is worth fighting to protect."

"I'm glad you are here, old friend."

"That's what brothers are for," Durov replied, patting Thane hard on the back as he tried to move a chess piece illegally without being caught.

"I saw that."

Durov grinned, shrugging. "It was worth a shot."

Lilly was allowed to awaken once they had literally reached the end of the road. The rest of the two-day journey would be on foot.

This was the designated transfer point.

Lilly opened her eyes slowly and then whined when she realized who was standing above her.

"Are you wondering why you are still alive?" Thane asked. "My friend wants you dead, and I know you would not hesitate to do the same to him."

"But never you, Thane. I love you too much to hurt you."

A few simple words from her mouth, and he was ready to strangle her.

"It's a dog eat dog world, correct?"

Her jaw dropped. Looking around the desolated landscape she cried, "Are you going to kill me here?"

"There is not one redeemable thing about you but, for some reason, my wife has decided to spare your life."

Lilly's eyes lit up, thinking she'd been given a reprieve.

"Consider this," he continued. "The woman you

wanted to sell into slavery is responsible for saving your life. You may consider it a weakness on her part, but the truth is she is far stronger than either you or I. She has earned my admiration and love, and *that* is the only reason I am honoring her wish by sparing your life now."

Lilly stood up, staring at Durov warily. She scanned the barren countryside. "Where are we? You aren't going to leave me here, are you?" She turned on Durov. "How is that any better than killing me outright? You fucking coward!"

Durov said nothing but smashed his fist into his palm.

"We are leaving you here, but you will not be alone." Thane pointed to a small group making their way to them.

Without warning, Durov ripped off Lilly's clothes and pushed her to the ground. "You will meet your fate as naked as the day you were born," he snarled.

She turned to Thane. "What the hell is this?"

"I'm giving you a second chance, which is far more than you deserve."

When Lilly tried to run, Durov pressed his boot into the middle of her back, holding her down in the dirt while they waited for the party to approach.

One woman walked ahead of the group, her hands pressed together in prayer. She was followed by several other nuns and three men hefting large backpacks for the journey.

She nodded to Durov when she approached. He immediately took his foot off Lilly, and smiled at her self-consciously.

"Miss Meyers, I have come to offer you redemption."

Lilly stood up slowly, not bothering to cover up her nakedness as she stared at the woman with contempt. "I don't want your redemption," she answered, spitting on the ground.

The nun eyed her for several moments before stating, "You cannot know what you need if you have never experienced it."

"Well, I know I don't need anything from *you*." She turned to face Durov. "Just get it over with, damn it."

Durov smiled. "*Nyet.*"

She focused on Thane, pleading "Don't you dare leave me here. Don't do to me what you did to our mother."

Unlike Ruth, Thane was certain he would feel zero remorse if Lilly died in this place. "You are being given a chance. What you choose to do with it is up to you."

The Reverend Mother gazed into Thane's eyes for several moments before speaking. "Mr. Davis, it is my honor and God-given duty to care for this lost soul."

"The fuck it is!" Lilly howled, lunging at her. She was stopped in her tracks when the Reverend Mother produced a cane from her loose sleeve and rapped Lilly hard on the head.

Lilly fell to her knees, stunned by the impact.

"You are but a wayward child in the eyes of the Lord and shall be treated as such."

The Reverend Mother turned to address Durov. "I appreciate the challenge you have offered me. Know that it will be handled with care."

He bowed his head to her. "Thank you, Mother Yana."

"Yes. Thank you, Reverend Mother," Thane said, bowing his head as well. "I hope you can make a difference with her."

Lilly rubbed the lump forming on her forehead and hissed. "I'm not fucking going anywhere with you fucking nut jobs."

The other nuns produced canes and encircled her.

"God chose you, Miss Meyers. I am but an instrument of His will."

Lilly looked through the circle of nuns at Thane, a terrified look on her face. "Don't leave me with these crazy women. I'll fucking gut them if you do."

All five nuns whacked Lilly with their canes, causing her to scream out in pain.

"Unwholesome speech is not tolerated, Miss Meyers. Every word, every thought, must glorify the Lord."

"You're speaking crazy talk!" Lilly cried. "Thane, you can't do this. I'm your sister, for God's sake!"

The Reverend Mother rapped her mouth with her cane. "You are only allowed to speak to me from now on."

Lilly grasped her jaw, howling again.

"Silence."

When the Reverend Mother raised her cane, Lilly instantly became mute.

Addressing the two men, she said, "She is my charge now. You have been released from the burden."

Thane suddenly felt the dark rage in his heart lifting as if it had been physically taken from him. He gasped in response.

The Reverend Mother nodded to him before turning back to Lilly. "Come, Miss Meyers, It's time to put away your childish ways and start anew."

Lilly cried out Thane's name, begging him not to leave her.

He walked away, hearing the satisfying crack of the cane as she was corrected.

"Disobedience will not be tolerated," the Reverend Mother scolded in a calm voice. "Now, get up and be grateful for the Lord's mercy."

Thane shot a glance at Durov. "You were right. Mother Yana is perfect."

The Russian grunted in agreement. "I leave with a content heart."

"As do I, brother."

Thane pressed the ring on his finger, relishing the feel of Brie's steady heartbeat.

I'm coming home, babygirl.

His Goddess

"And now, téa, this man is going to think of you as a goddess even as I fuck you like a slut."

Brie was on her hands and knees on the bed, naked before him. She turned her head, looking back at him hungrily and purred, "Yes, Master."

Thane felt the rush of sexual domination as he grabbed her hips and forcefully thrust his cock into her. She cried out as her body took that first solid stroke.

God, it had been so long since he'd heard that sound come from her lips. It spurred him on as he let his primal urges take over. Thane grabbed a fistful of her hair and pulled her head back.

"Are you ready to be thoroughly fucked, my dear?"

She arched her back and begged, "Please, Master."

With one hand pulling on her hair and the other grasping her waist, he began stroking his submissive with his cock, standing fully upright and in charge.

Thane felt like a kid in a candy store as he tried various positions with her.

Brie on her back, legs spread wide.

Brie straddling the tantra chair, back arched.

Brie with her knees together, ass in the air.

Brie bound in cuffs, hands above her head.

By the time he was done, she was left weak and trembling. It was then that he commanded she kneel on the floor to wait for him.

Thane left to wash, taking his time as he cleaned himself thoroughly. When he returned, he smiled down at Brie.

Lightly tracing her lips with his finger, he asked, "Do you remember your first lesson with me and this beautiful mouth of yours?"

She looked up at him, her eyes full of amorous lust. "I do, Master."

"I remember it very well. In fact, I've been anticipating fucking your face for quite some time now."

"You have?" she asked, obviously pleased.

"I have, babygirl…" He held out a strand of red satin and knelt behind her. "Wrists."

Brie dutifully put her hands behind her back, and he bound them together. After he'd made sure his tie was secure, Thane stood back up and admired his gift to himself. Running his hand through her hair, he murmured, "You are a beautiful thing."

Brie looked up at him, her nipples hard and her eyes luminous.

Stroking his cock, he looked at his goddess, admiring those big honey-colored eyes, those pink, full lips, and the long, dark curls that framed that exquisite face. Truly, she was a classic beauty and, fortunately for him, she craved his kinky desires.

"Open yourself to me, téa."

She obediently opened her lips, gazing up at him in adoration.

Thane gathered her hair up with one hand and used it to guide her mouth onto his cock. He gradually forced her lips farther down his shaft. "First, my dear, we will start off gentle, and then I'll give it to you rough."

Brie moaned in pleasure as she relaxed her throat. He began slowly thrusting his shaft deeper. "Nice..." he complimented her as he watched her mouth drip with saliva, his thrusts becoming longer and more powerful with each stroke.

The erotic vision of his shaft disappearing into her mouth as she looked up at him was inspiring. "I won't hold back."

She broke away long enough to say, "Thank you, Master."

He regathered her hair. "Open wide. I plan to thoroughly enjoy that lusty throat of yours."

Thane forced his cock deep, reveling in the tight constriction. Brie took each thrust, her gaze never leaving his as he fucked her face with abandon. Watching her take it proved too much as the intense ache of his building orgasm reached its peak. Thane cried out, his entire body shuddering in release. With great satisfaction, he held her head still as he pumped his essence deep into her throat.

"Fuck..." he cried out in a masculine roar of satisfaction.

Brie disengaged and grinned up at him.

"I have something else for you," he informed her.

Thane left Brie momentarily, returning with her white strand of pearls—the ones that seemed to have a cursed history between them. Tonight, he would lift the curse and restore them to their rightful place.

He had Brie lay on the tantra chair and spread her legs wide. He smiled in admiration as he looked down at her red pussy, swollen with use.

"You know what's about to happen?"

She nodded eagerly, biting her lip in anticipation.

Separating her wet pussy lips, Thane placed the pearls on either side of her clit. Pulling the necklace taut, he watched her squirm in pleasure as he dragged them down slowly, her clit dancing to the caress of the pearls. He did it several times, enjoying her reaction.

It brought back memories of when he had played her Khan during the final week of training. That night, she'd made the mistake that turned out to be his salvation—when she'd spoken those three dangerous words, "I love you".

Although he had immediately ended their evening together, her declaration of love had remained with him and eventually changed the course of his life.

He leaned down and said to her what he could not that night, "I am deeply in love with you, Brie."

She lifted her chin and kissed him. "I'm in love with you, too."

He laid the strand of pearls on her pregnant stomach in a concentric circle and admired her decorated belly. "You always looked sexy in pearls."

Brie smiled as she stared at the necklace. "This was the first gift you ever gave me."

"These babies have had a bad history between us, but they were meant as a token of my sincerest admiration."

She picked them up and pressed the pearls against her chest. "I'll admit I may have had a love/hate relationship with them, but I still cherished them because they came from you."

"And now you can associate them with tonight."

She lifted her head and slipped them on, letting the pearls settle between her breasts. "Thank you for this beautiful gift, then and now."

Thane stared at her. Truly, there was nothing in the world more beautiful than this woman. He leaned down and kissed her tenderly.

"My goddess."

Durov had rescheduled the operation but had only shared the date and time with Thane. "I do not want *radost moya* anywhere near the hospital. There are too many germs there, and I know she will not stay away even if I forbid it."

"She will not be happy, old friend," Thane warned.

"Ah, but she will," he insisted. "I have planned a special gift for both her and you."

"We don't need anything."

"But you will appreciate it," he said with a smile. "And she will *love* it. Trust me."

"What if something happens to you?"

Durov shrugged. "There will be nothing you can do. Better I do this alone. You come visit me at the beach house after a few days."

"I had assumed you'd stay with us."

"*Nyet*, comrade. I do not want her fussing over me when she should be taking care of herself and *moye solntse*. I have hired medical staff to care for me so I can recover quickly like you did."

Thane looked at him with concern.

"I will be fine."

"If anything should happen, Brie will—"

"I have made my decision. If anyone questions it, they can answer to me later."

Thane grabbed him in a firm embrace. "My thoughts will be with you."

"Thank you, brother."

"Look who decided to surprise us, Sir!"

Durov's gift arrived the day of his surgery and came in the form of Tono Nosaka.

The look on Brie's face when she opened the door and found Nosaka and Autumn standing in the doorway was priceless.

"What the heck are you guys doing in town?" she cried, hugging them both before ushering them inside.

Nosaka shook Thane's hand while Autumn gushed over Brie.

"You look positively radiant with motherhood,

Brie."

Brie looked down at her large belly. "Radiant and huge."

Nosaka smiled at her tenderly. "Durov flew us in today to capture your motherhood for all eternity."

"What do you mean?" she laughed, glancing at Thane to see if he knew anything about this. He shook his head, although he had a good idea what Durov had planned.

"I'll be taking pictures of you today and creating a decorative wax mold of your stomach." He turned to Thane. "With your permission, of course."

"You not only have my permission, but also my gratitude."

"Wonderful. Autumn and I will get the equipment out of our rental and set things up. Mr. Davis, you will be part of the shoot, as well, so please dress formally."

"What would you like me to wear, Tono?" Brie asked.

"A favorite outfit, and a flattering bra and panty set. I will be taking both traditional shots and ones that show off your bare stomach."

"Nosaka."

"Yes, Sir Davis."

"I would also like photos of Brie completely nude with nothing to distract from her natural beauty."

Brie blushed, looking at him in adoration.

She turned to Autumn and asked, "Are you okay with that?"

Autumn's smile was genuine as she stared tenderly at Brie. "I have no issues, my friend. I think these photos will be stunning."

Brie looked at Thane, her eyes reflecting her inner excitement. "I can't believe Rytsar did this! We should invite him to come over and watch." She grabbed her phone to call him.

Nosaka spoke up. "Actually, Brie, he wanted to be surprised by the photos we take. I am supposed to make a set of copies for both you and him."

Brie grinned at Sir. "Well, there's no harm in thanking him, at least." She dialed his cell and frowned when he didn't answer. "Hey, Rytsar, I was hoping to thank you for this wonderful gift, but am leaving you a message, instead. We'll be sure to take a photo especially for you."

While Nosaka and Autumn set up for the photo shoot, Thane and Brie readied themselves. Brie swept back her hair and secured it with the orchid comb Nosaka had given her, so that her curls tumbled down her back in waves.

"Very nice," Thane complimented her as he tightened the knot of his tie. "I want to discuss a few ideas I have with Nosaka while you finish dressing. No need to rush, babygirl."

"Thank you, Sir," she said, beaming at him.

While Nosaka was setting up, Thane explained to him, "After you finish the shots of Brie and I together, I will be leaving to check on Durov."

Nosaka was about to protest, but Thane stopped him. "Yes, I understand he said he didn't want visitors, but I know him. He is terrified of hospitals, and I'm not going to let him face this alone no matter how much he fights me on it."

Nosaka nodded. "Say no more. You are a good friend, Sir Davis."

Brie came out from the back looking like the goddess she was. Regal and dignified, with a minimum of makeup to keep an air of youthful charm.

"I'm so excited about doing this," she confessed. "Not only do I get pictures and wax, but I also get to spend the day with you two. This is such a wonderful surprise!"

Nosaka gazed at her, his voice warm with affection. "It is a pleasure and honor to be here today for such a happy occasion."

"Things have definitely improved since the last time you were here. Thank you, Tono. For everything," Brie said, her voice heavy with emotion.

Nosaka turned his gaze to Thane. "I always remained confident you would recover. You have a strong spirit and a devoted heart."

Thane nodded, appreciating the man's wisdom and influence in their lives. "I am grateful Durov thought to call you. It gives me a chance to formally thank you for what you did for Brie while I was in the coma."

Nosaka picked up his camera and adjusted it, smiling at Thane. "What I did I considered a privilege because I think so highly of you two. It fortifies my heart to see you both now, whole and content."

Nosaka asked Autumn to adjust the angle of one of the lights and then said, "Sir Davis, would you stand behind Brie and wrap your arms around her, placing your hands on her stomach…"

Thane left an hour later, pleased with the photos Nosaka had taken so far, including the one with Brie sitting on the floor naked, the infamous vodka bottle with the red line through it in-between her legs, artfully hiding her pubic region.

Before Thane left, he asked Nosaka privately, "Would you bind her belly in a decorative pattern? Your work is exquisite, and I know she will enjoy it."

"Certainly, Sir Davis."

Thane went directly to the hospital and met Durov in the prep room he'd been put in before surgery. The Russian's face lit up the moment he saw Thane walking through the door, but then he frowned angrily.

"*Moy droog*, you are not supposed to be here. Go home and enjoy my gift."

"I am not leaving you, old friend. Like it or not, you're stuck with me."

Durov turned his head away and growled, "This is totally unnecessary."

Thane could hear the fear in his voice that he was trying desperately to hide. This was not a simple dislike for doctors, but the deep-seated belief that he would die in this place. Thane knew this, and put his hand on Durov's shoulder to reassure him. "There is no shame in feeling troubled, brother. I hate this place, too. But you will leave here with your broken ribs mended. It won't be long before you are swinging your cat o' nines again."

Durov turned his head toward him. "I want to pick the babe up and dance with her without pain."

"Yes, because the last thing you want to be is a *dyadya* who grimaces whenever you cradle her."

"That would be a great tragedy."

"It would."

A nurse came in holding a tray with a syringe. "It's time, Mr. Durov. The shot will help you relax before we wheel you into the operating room. Can you hold out your left arm for me, please?"

Durov glanced at Thane.

"You've got this."

With bravery only Thane understood, his friend held his arm out and surrendered to his greatest fear.

Here

"Durov isn't doing well."

"What do you mean?" Brie cried.

"It's only been a week, and he pushed himself too hard. Now he's been relegated to bed rest. Needless to say, he's in a *foul* mood."

"We should go cheer him up, then."

Thane gave her an amused look. "You haven't experienced Durov at his worst."

"I'm not scared."

He chuckled. "Well...you should be."

Thane agreed that a visit was definitely in order and decided to take his Lotus for the trip. It had been far too long since he'd been behind the wheel, and with a child on the way, who knew how long he would have the chance?

Brie was thrilled he was taking the Lotus Evora for a spin, but needed his help easing into it. She looked up at him gratefully once she was settled in the red leather seat. "I just love this hot car."

"Shall I make her fly for you?"

Brie grinned as he got into it. "Oh, Sir, this reminds me of old times."

Thane winked at her, suddenly seeing the nervous young woman she'd been that first car ride with him.

He tested the vehicle around a few corners before pushing the gas. Brie squealed beside him, begging Thane to go faster. Being familiar with the car, he had complete confidence as he opened her up and let his Lotus fly.

Thankfully, the freeway traffic was abnormally light, allowing for a satisfying drive for them both. When he finally pulled up to Durov's place, he was feeling exhilarated and alive—like he had been before the crash.

Looking at Brie, he could tell she was feeling the same.

"Almost a shame Rytsar doesn't live farther away," she giggled as he helped her out of the car. Looking at her belly, it amazed him to think that in a few more weeks, the bump she carried would be gone and they would be holding a tiny human.

Thane rang the doorbell and heard angry grumbles emanating from the interior of the house. Maxim answered the door a few minutes later with a tight expression. "I apologize. We aren't taking visitors right now."

Brie giggled, pushing her way through the door. "We aren't visitors. We're family."

When Thane entered the room, he saw Durov laying prostrate on the couch, Little Sparrow on the ground at his feet. The dogs ears were laid back and her eyes wide with worry as she stared at her Master. She did not wag her tail or acknowledge them in any way as Thane and Brie approached, her attention riveted solely on Durov.

Durov, however, attempted to get up and let loose a string of Russian curses as he did so.

"Don't you dare stand up," Brie scolded. "Your stubbornness is what got you into this situation in the first place."

Durov shot her a hostile glare, but took his anger out on Thane.

"I was promised quick recovery, comrade, but look at me! Ordered to stay in bed?" He smashed his fist into his hand and glowered at Thane as if he were to blame.

Brie walked over, pushing Durov back down on the couch as she *tsked* at him gently. "If you want to slow down the healing process, just keep doing what you're doing, Rytsar."

"I am a man, *radost moya*, not a potato."

"You will behave like a good potato until Dr. Hessen says otherwise."

"*Nyet*. I will not!"

Thane smirked at Durov. "You suck as a patient, old friend."

Durov snarled. "I blame this on you."

"How so?"

"You pushed your body, and look where it got you." He motioned his hand up and down at Thane, then pointed to himself. "I do the same and am punished for it."

Thane raised an eyebrow. "It's only been a week. I'm pretty sure you were told to rest."

"I have no time with the babe coming. I must be

healed."

"Then take my advice. Listen to the medical professionals you hired and do *exactly* what they tell you. Trust me, it'll work."

Durov harrumphed.

"Rytsar, you vowed you would be the best *dyadya*. So that means you have to stay in bed." Brie patted her stomach, grinning at him. "Do you really want to break your promise to her?"

"That is a low blow, *radost moya*," he growled bitterly.

While Thane appreciated Brie's approach, he was uncertain it would help, considering Durov's current mood.

Brie met Durov's harsh gaze, looking at him with compassion.

Little Sparrow whined.

Thane glanced at Maxim, who shook his head.

Brie suddenly stood up and announced, "I know exactly what you need."

She walked slowly to the kitchen, bearing the weight of her late-term pregnancy.

"Did you notice the change in her belly?" Durov asked Thane when she was out of earshot.

"Yes, I've noticed she's dropped recently." He added with a smirk, "Which means you don't have long to recover."

Durov frowned. "But I cannot tolerate being in bed."

"Says the man with metal screws in his chest."

"Leave me alone, comrade," Durov growled irritably. "I am not in the mood."

Brie walked back in with a bottle of vodka in one hand and three glasses in the other.

Thane was taken aback. "Are you planning to drink, babygirl?"

"Nope," she answered coyly as she poured the vodka into three glasses.

She handed the first one to Thane, the second to Durov, then folded her hands in her lap.

"Drink up, boys," she told them with a wink.

Thane hadn't touched any alcohol since promising Brie to abstain from it. "Are you sure?" he asked. "I'm a man of my word."

"Yes," she answered. "While I sincerely appreciate your dedication to me, your brother needs a drinking buddy right now."

"And the third glass?" Durov asked, staring at it and then her.

Brie only answered with a smile.

"I am suspicious of your woman's silence," Durov grumbled.

"I'm curious about it, as well," Thane replied, looking at Brie.

"Trust me," she told them both as she pushed off the chair and waddled into the kitchen.

"Let's toss back a quick one and refill it before she returns," Durov said with a mischievous grin, sounding like a naughty child.

Thane found it oddly amusing and clinked glasses before downing it. He had both glasses refilled before Brie came back, carrying another shot glass filled to the brim with water.

"What are you two grinning about?" she asked as she settled into her chair.

Durov leaned toward her and whispered, "I was just telling your man how attractive you are when you waddle."

Her mouth dropped. "You didn't just go there."

"I find it utterly charming, *radost moya*."

Brie shook her head. "Only you could say something insulting and make it adorably sweet."

Durov grinned and held up his glass to her.

"Can I make the toast?" Brie asked.

"But of course."

"Here's to the unexpected." She raised her glass to them both.

Thane smiled as he held up his glass and downed his second drink.

While Brie was filling up their glasses, the doorbell rang and she called out in a singsongy voice, "I'll get it."

"Do you see it, comrade?" Durov commented in a voice loud enough for her to hear. "The way she gracefully sways like a penguin."

Brie turned her head and shot him a look.

"You're skating on thin ice, my friend," Thane warned, chuckling to himself. He relaxed, sitting back in his chair, enjoying the warmth of the drink as it flowed through his veins. It had been a while since he'd had any alcohol, and he seemed to be unusually sensitive to it...

High-pitched squeals filled the front foyer.

Durov perked up on the couch and asked in a concerned voice, "Is that who I think it is, *moy droog?*"

Little Sparrow whined softly, nudging her head under

his hand, responding to his discomfort.

"I have a joke about pizza…" echoed from the foyer in answer. "Oh, wait, it's too cheesy."

"Yes, my friend, I believe it is."

Brie burst out laughing as she ushered Lea into the room. "Oh, my goodness, Lea. That was *great!*"

Durov looked pensive as the two girls walked toward him.

Thane wondered if Brie's idea of a little pick-me-up for Durov was about to explode in her face.

Brie sat Lea beside her and handed her friend the other shot glass.

"See, girlfriend, I saved the last shot for you."

Lea picked it up and beamed a charming smile at Durov. "I've got a joke for you, Rytsar Durov."

"Ms. Taylor, there is no need," he assured her.

"Ah, but there is. I saved it especially for you."

"Don't do it," he warned.

"I'm going to anyway."

"*Nyet.*"

"I must," she said, grinning.

The girl reminded Thane of an insect who had to fly into the light no matter the consequences.

"Do it like a band-aid, Rytsar," Brie advised. "Let her tell you the punch line, and then down a shot of vodka afterward."

Durov glanced over at Thane and grumbled. "I'm only consenting because there is vodka involved."

"Hold up your glasses, everyone," Lea cried out eagerly, giggling before she even began. "If you're European on the toilet, what are you on the way to the bathroom?"

Durov shook his head. When she turned to Thane, he only gave a slight shrug.

"Brie?" Lea asked.

Not even waiting for her to answer, Lea blurted, "You're a Russian!" and howled with laughter.

Durov immediately swallowed his shot, with Thane finishing right after.

Lea beamed at them, still holding her glass up, waiting for a reaction.

Durov was silent as he leaned forward, grabbing the bottle and pouring both Thane and himself another shot. They chugged together, setting the glasses on the table in silence afterward.

"Come on…it was funny," Lea insisted. She turned to Brie for confirmation, but Brie had her eyes locked on Durov.

Lea's gaze darted over to Thane, and she gave him a questioning look, clearly wondering if she had said something wrong.

"Ms. Taylor," Durov stated, finally breaking the uncomfortable silence.

"Yes?" she asked, when he said nothing more.

He took a long breath, letting it out slowly, a single chuckle escaping his stern lips.

Lea cracked a hopeful smile.

"Eur-o-pean," he repeated slowly in his thick Russian accent, emphasizing the *pean,* when he said it.

Brie's cheeks turned bright red before she burst out in a fit of giggles.

Lea joined her, and their infectious merriment caused

Rytsar to laugh out loud. He immediately groaned in pain as he grabbed his chest.

Durov's discomfort set Thane off, and he let out a low roll of laughter. He blamed it on the vodka, but did not protest when Durov poured him another.

For the first time Little Sparrow wagged her tail, hopping excitedly as she let out small yips at her Master. Durov held out his hand and she rushed to it, wiggling in delight when he began stroking her head.

The doorbell rang and Brie immediately piped up, "I'll get it!" as she headed toward the door.

Thane wasn't sure what Brie was up to, but it seemed she was weaving some kind of magic spell based on the relaxed expression Durov now wore.

Two new guests entered the room. When Rytsar saw the couple, he bellowed, "Nosaka!"

The Asian Dom gave him a slight bow, then bowed to Thane.

"What are you doing here?" Durov asked good-naturedly.

Nosaka glanced at Brie. "Mrs. Davis indicated we were invited."

"And you are, Tono," Brie assured him as she waddled over to the couple. "It's my surprise for Rytsar."

"*Moy droog*, did you know anything about this?"

Thane shook his head.

"Would you like us to leave?" Autumn asked, blushing in embarrassment.

"*Nyet!*" Durov cried out warmly, "More vodka for everyone." He then pointed at Brie and added, "Except for you, *radost moya*."

She pouted with her bottom lip.

Thane started to stand up, wanting to greet the two, but Nosaka shook his head. "No need to stand for family."

Thane inclined his head to them both and settled back in his chair.

The doorbell rang again as Maxim walked into the room with another bottle of vodka and two more shot glasses for Nosaka and Autumn.

Thane was pleased to see Baron, Captain and Candy join the impromptu gathering. He watched in amusement as Maxim did an about-face and headed back into the kitchen for more shot glasses.

As more people came, the vodka began to flow freely, but it didn't start getting interesting until Wallace showed up with Kylie in tow. Wallace entered the room, sporting a black business suit with an eyepatch to match. Rather than being self-conscious about the missing eye, Wallace was embracing it, making it a part of his persona. Because many knew the circumstances behind his injury, it set him apart as an honored member of the BDSM community.

However, the conversation surrounding his missing eye took an unexpected turn when Wallace mentioned he was about to visit his parents in Colorado. "They don't know anything about this," he said, pointing to his face. "And I'm not planning on telling them what really happened. My poor mother would totally pass out, after having already survived my kidney transplant last year."

"So, what are you going to tell them?" Baron asked.

Wallace downed a shot, grinning as he set it down. "I

was toying with, 'Hey, Mom, you know how you always said not to run with scissors?'"

Several people chuckled.

"I'm open to suggestions, though," he said, glancing around the room. "Seriously." When no one spoke, he asked, "Anyone…anyone…?"

Lea raised her hand.

"Hit me, Lea."

"Mom, I tried my hand at juggling with knives, and we can all see how that turned out."

Someone gasped, possibly thinking it hit too close to home, but Wallace laughed. "There we go! That's what I'm talking about…"

Rytsar took the bait. "Mother, I was curious about the suction level of a breast pump and got too close."

Wallace laughed even harder, pouring them both a shot and toasting the Russian's contribution.

That's when the vodka really began to flow as people suggested outlandish excuses to explain Wallace's missing eye—from a fistfight in an all-male biker bar to a paintball accident, and even an erection machine gone horribly wrong.

The entire room was rolling with laughter by the time Wallace finally called it quits. "I stuck a fork in it and we're done!" he announced.

The entire room exploded in inebriated laughter.

Brie was laughing with the rest of them, exclaiming, "That was so, so wrong."

While the room was still erupting in bursts of laughter, a new visitor called out over the din. "What's a girl gotta do to get attention around here?"

The room suddenly fell silent.

Thane turned to the familiar voice, grateful Brie had thought to invite her.

Only a handful of people knew the great risk Mary had taken for Brie, so she was greeted with glares from those who were resentful over her harsh breakup with Wallace—a man who now held the respect of everyone in attendance.

There was a moment of uneasiness before Brie broke the silence. "Mary Quite Contrary, you finally came!" She made her way to Mary, throwing her arms around her friend.

"Oh, Lord, woman, you are *huge*. What do you have in there? Twins?" Mary asked, gawking at Brie's stomach.

Lea growled under her breath, "Blonde Nemesis…"

Several people in the room shifted uncomfortably.

Rytsar instantly changed the dynamic in the room by stating enthusiastically, "I wish, because it would make me a double *dyadya*."

A few chuckles followed his comment.

Thane stood up and beckoned Mary to him. "Miss Wilson, it's a pleasure to see you again."

Mary oozed across the floor with sexual grace.

Thane understood that she relied on her feminine appeal whenever she found herself in uncomfortable situations—and he did not want her to feel uneasy now. Not in a room of her peers and friends.

He took her hand in his and clasped it firmly. Thane wanted the entire room to know about his high regard for her.

The conversations in the room suddenly started up

again as if a spell had been broken.

"I am glad you came," he told her, squeezing her hand before he let her go.

"Of course, Sir Davis. When Brie told me there was going to be free booze, there was no way I was staying away."

"You should speak to Mr. Wallace," he told her in a low voice. "I think it will ease the tension in the room."

Although everyone had reacted to Mary's entrance, Thane had taken note of how tense Kylie seemed now. While it was absolutely necessary for Wallace to keep Mary's secret from her, it put the two of them in an awkward dynamic that he hoped a simple public interaction might remedy.

While Mary was speaking to them both, Baron took the opportunity to talk to Thane with Captain by his side. "Do you remember the meeting we set up before your trip to Dubai?"

"I certainly do."

"Would you like to know what the two of us have been doing ever since?"

"Naturally." Thane gestured to Brie to join him, suspecting it had something to do with their wedding gift.

Baron smiled as Brie approached. "Please join us, kitten. What I have to share is for both your ears."

His mysterious smile was infectious. "The house I bought in Adrianna's and my old neighborhood held a surprise I wasn't expecting."

"What?" Brie asked excitedly.

"It turns out that my home used to be a secret dungeon. Even the realtor was unaware at the time of the sale. I became curious when the basement seemed off from the rest of the house. Studying the original floor plans, I realized they did not match up. With a little investigation and a sledge hammer, I uncovered an entire dungeon, complete with an antique St. Andrew's Cross, whipping poles, and an entire wall covered in a mosaic of erotic scenes of Rome."

Thane shook his head. "Amazing that no one knew about it."

"I agree," Baron replied. "I find the history of this secret BDSM community fascinating, and wanted to put the house to good use. That's when I contacted Captain."

Captain nodded at Thane. "Both Baron and I have an interest in helping people in the community who have been abused by those in authority. We never refer to our clients as victims because our goal is to help them reassert their power."

"What a worthy endeavor," Brie complimented. "I can't think of two people better suited for it."

"Actually…" Baron began, looking at both Brie and Thane. "We were hoping you both would consider joining us."

Thane cocked his head. "In what capacity?"

"As instructors. We not only want to help these submissives heal, but to experience firsthand what healthy D/s relationships look like before, during, and after a scene."

Thane had to admit he was interested in the prospect of teaching again, but was unsure why they were asking him when both men were qualified for such a position.

"Can't you do that with Candy?" Thane asked Captain.

"Since Candy will be working alongside both Baron and I, we feel it is important to keep our roles as strictly advocates for our submissives, rather than act as their instructors."

Thane noticed Brie staring at him intently.

"What is it, Brie?"

"I have longed for an opportunity like this for you, Sir. Ever since you gave up your position as Headmaster of the Center, in fact. You were always meant to teach."

He put his arm around her. "I do not need it to be satisfied with my life."

"I'm not just thinking of you, but of the students who would benefit from your instruction."

By then, Candy had joined them and told Brie, "You would be an important part of it, too, sharing your perspective and experiences as a submissive during the sessions."

Brie smiled. "It reminds me of the lessons Tono and I taught together."

"Similar, yes," Thane agreed. "And you said you enjoyed the experience."

"Very much, Sir." Brie took his hand and looked up at him. "What an honor it would be to work beside you while helping submissives reclaim their power."

"A worthy endeavor, indeed."

"Is that a yes?" Baron asked with a grin.

Durov roared from the couch, "Did I just hear someone offer my comrade a teaching position?"

Everyone turned to Thane, clearly excited.

Thane smiled at the group, answering smoothly, "Discussing possibilities, nothing more."

"Let's toast to your future, *moy droog*," Durov insisted.

Another round of vodka was consumed.

Finishing his shot, Thane told Baron, "Ask me again after the baby is born and we have adjusted to family life."

"Of course," Baron agreed, winking at Brie.

Captain took Thane's hand and shook it firmly. "I look forward to discussing this more in depth with you at a later date."

"As do I, Captain."

Thane looked around the room, impressed with the people Brie had managed to gather on such short notice. Mr. Gallant and his wife caught his eye, and he walked over to them.

"Mrs. Gallant, it is always a pleasure when we meet."

The stunning Amazonian woman bowed her head respectfully. "I feel the same, Sir Davis."

Thane turned to Gallant. "Have you heard the proposal Baron and Captain are suggesting?"

"Yes. Captain and I are good friends and often confide in each other."

"I respect your opinion, Gallant. Any thoughts?"

"You and Mrs. Davis would work well in such an environment."

"Even with a child?"

Mr. Gallant smiled. "If it is worth doing, you will find a way. Ena and I have found that to be the case."

"Yes, it's true," Thane agreed. "You two are proof

that a BDSM couple can make it work with a family."

Mr. Gallant gazed at him intently. "I have always respected you, Sir Davis. And you know that I admire Brie. This opportunity seems like a good fit for your talents and heart."

"I apprecia—"

Brie burst out in laughter talking to Lea and Mary, but it was cut short when she suddenly got an odd expression on her face. She looked over at Thane, blushing profusely. "I think I just laughed so hard I peed."

She looked down at the floor in humiliation. Thane followed her gaze saw a puddle of clear water on the floor.

"Mrs. Davis, I'm fairly certain that's not pee," Ena told her.

Brie looked at her with a confused expression.

Ena smiled warmly, and explained, "I believe your water just broke."

"Sir…" Brie whimpered, looking to Thane.

The possibility that she would deliver early had not occurred to him. Thane's heart started racing.

The time is here…

"How are you feeling?" he immediately asked her, the Dominant in him kicking in.

"I'm green, Sir," she giggled. "No labor pains at all."

"Perfectly normal," Ena assured her. "But you'll need to get to the hospital."

Brie shot Thane a worried glance. "But I'm not due for another three weeks!"

Thane was already on the phone, calling her obstetrician. He struggled to hear the doctor's instructions over Durov's loud bellowing.

"*Moye solntse* can't come. I haven't healed yet!"

Thane covered the phone and gave him a stern look. "She *is* coming. So get your ass ready, old friend. We're heading to the hospital."

The entire room burst into excited chatter.

Thane's aunt moved over to Brie and gave her a nurturing hug. "Let's get you to the restroom and freshen up so you can have this baby." She gently guided Brie out of the room with Ena following close behind.

"Nothing to worry about," Ena assured Brie with a tender smile. "The same thing happened with my first child…"

Thane felt momentarily lost, unprepared for it to happen three weeks early—and certainly not during a drunken party at the beach.

Gallant put a firm hand on his shoulder. "Everything will be fine. They'll induce her now that the water has broken. Within the next 48 hours, you will be a father."

Father…

As Thane took that in, everything seemed to instantly fall back into place.

"Maxim, I need you to prepare a large thermos of coffee, and get Durov in the car," he ordered.

"Unc, can you go to my place and get Brie's overnight bag? We left it in the front hall. Oh, and please check on the cat."

"Of course, Thane. We'll be happy to."

"Wallace, can you take my car back to our apartment? We'll be riding with Rytsar's entourage."

Wallace looked stunned. "You're letting me drive your Lotus?"

"Of course. You even have my permission to take Kylie for a spin before you park her in the garage. A car like that needs to be appreciated."

Turning to Gray, knowing Brie's father held him in high esteem, Thane asked, "Could you call Brie's parents and help them make arrangements to come out?"

"Certainly, Sir Davis."

Thane looked at Brie and time seemed to stop.

Their lives were about to drastically change.

Brie looked uncertain, thrown off by the unexpected timing of the birth.

He smiled confidently, holding out his hand to her. "Come with me, Brie."

Her countenance suddenly changed as she took his hand and met his gaze. Thane was reminded of her on collaring night, when he'd helped her out of the elevator after giving up his career at the Training Center.

Now, just like then, a new world was opening up before him and his life would never be the same.

Thane was ready to embrace it—with all its uncertainties and complications.

He had been given this rare second chance...

Against all odds, Thane was about to meet his little girl.

Thank you so much for reading. I hope you enjoyed the 16th book in the Brie's Submission series. The journey continues in ***Bound by Love***.

My dear fans,
The adventure isn't over yet!
Get ready for the next part of the story –
told through Brie's point of view.
This is going to be a joyous celebration for the Submissive Training Center gang! ~Red
(Release Date – March 20, 2018)

COMING NEXT

Bound by Love: Brie's Submission

17th Book in the Series

Available for Preorder

Reviews mean the world to me!

I truly appreciate you taking the time to review
In Sir's Arms.

If you could leave a review on both Goodreads and the
site where you purchased this book from, I would be so
grateful. Sincerely, ~Red

ABOUT THE AUTHOR

Over Two Million readers have enjoyed Red's stories

Red Phoenix – USA Today Bestselling Author
Winner of 8 Readers' Choice Awards

Hey Everyone!

I'm Red Phoenix, an author who also happens to be a submissive in real life. I wrote the Brie's Submission series because I wanted people everywhere to know just how much fun BDSM can be.

There is a huge cast of characters who are part of Brie's journey. The further you read into the story the more you learn about each one. I hope you grow to love Brie and the gang as much as I do.

They've become like family.

When I'm not writing, you can find me online with readers.

I heart my fans! ~Red

To find out more visit my Website

redphoenix69.com

Follow Me on BookBub

bookbub.com/authors/red-phoenix

Newsletter: Sign up

redphoenix69.com/newsletter-signup

Facebook: RedPhoenix69

Twitter: @redphoenix69

Instagram: RedPhoenixAuthor

I invite you to join my reader Group!

facebook.com/groups/539875076052037

SIGN UP FOR MY NEWSLETTER
HERE FOR THE LATEST RED
PHOENIX UPDATES

SALES, GIVEAWAYS, NEW
RELEASES, EXCLUSIVE SNEAK
PEEKS, AND MORE!
SIGN UP HERE
REDPHOENIX69.COM/NEWSLETTER-SIGNUP

Red Phoenix is the author of:

Brie's Submission Series:
Teach Me #1
Love Me #2
Catch Me #3
Try Me #4
Protect Me #5
Hold Me #6
Surprise Me #7
Trust Me #8
Claim Me #9
Enchant Me #10
A Cowboy's Heart #11
Breathe with Me #12
Her Russian Knight #13
Under His Protection #14
Her Russian Returns #15
In Sir's Arms #16
Bound by Love #17 (3/20/2018)

***You can also purchase the
AUDIO BOOK Versions**

redphoenix69.com/reds-books/audio-books

Blissfully Undone
* Available in eBook and paperback

(Snowy Fun—Two people find themselves snowbound in a cabin where hidden love can flourish, taking one couple on a sensual journey into ménage à trois)

His Scottish Pet: Dom of the Ages
* Available in eBook and paperback

Audio Book: *His Scottish Pet: Dom of the Ages*

(Scottish Dom—A sexy Dom escapes to Scotland in the late 1400s. He encounters a waif who has the potential to free him from his tragic curse)

The Erotic Love Story of Amy and Troy
* Available in eBook and paperback

(Sexual Adventures—True love reigns, but fate continually throws Troy and Amy into the arms of others)

eBooks

Varick: The Reckoning

(Savory Vampire—A dark, sexy vampire story. The hero navigates the dangerous world he has been thrust into with lusty passion and a pure heart)

Keeper of the Wolf Clan (Keeper of Wolves, #1)

(Sexual Secrets—A virginal werewolf must act as the clan's mysterious Keeper)

The Keeper Finds Her Mate (Keeper of Wolves, #2)

(Second Chances—A young she-wolf must choose between old ties or new beginnings)

The Keeper Unites the Alphas (Keeper of Wolves, #3)

(Serious Consequences—The young she-wolf is captured by the rival clan)

Boxed Set: Keeper of Wolves Series (Books 1-3)

(Surprising Secrets—A secret so shocking it will rock Layla's world. The young she-wolf is put in a position of being able to save her werewolf clan or becoming the reason for its destruction)

Socrates Inspires Cherry to Blossom

(Satisfying Surrender—A mature and curvaceous woman becomes fascinated by an online Dom who has much to teach her)

By the Light of the Scottish Moon

(Saving Love—Two lost souls, the Moon, a werewolf, and a death wish…)

In 9 Days

(Sweet Romance—A young girl falls in love with the new student, nicknamed "the Freak")

9 Days and Counting

(Sacrificial Love—The sequel to *In 9 Days* delves into the emotional reunion of two longtime lovers)

And Then He Saved Me

(Saving Tenderness—When a young girl tries to kill herself, a man of great character intervenes with a love that heals)

Play With Me at Noon

(Seeking Fulfillment—A desperate wife lives out her fantasies by taking five different men in five days)

Connect with Red on Substance B

Substance B is a platform for independent authors to directly connect with their readers. Please visit Red's Substance B page where you can:

- Sign up for Red's newsletter
- Send a message to Red
- See all platforms where Red's books are sold

Visit Substance B today to learn more about your favorite independent authors.